P9-CQV-475

KILLING CUPID

Books by Laura Levine

THIS PEN FOR HIRE

LAST WRITES

KILLER BLONDE

SHOES TO DIE FOR

THE PMS MURDER

DEATH BY PANTYHOSE

CANDY CANE MURDER

KILLING BRIDEZILLA

KILLER CRUISE

DEATH OF A TROPHY WIFE

GINGERBREAD COOKIE MURDER

PAMPERED TO DEATH

DEATH OF A NEIGHBORHOOD WITCH

KILLING CUPID

Published by Kensington Publishing Corporation

A Jaine Austen Mystery

KILLING
CUPID

LAURA
LEVINE

KENSINGTON BOOKS
www.kensingtonbooks.com

KENSINGTON BOOKS are published by

Kensington Publishing Corp.
119 West 40th Street
New York, NY 10018

All Kensington titles, imprints and distributed lines are available at special quantity discounts for bulk purchases for sales promotion, premiums, fund-raising, educational or institutional use.

Special book excerpts or customized printings can also be created to fit specific needs. For details, write or phone the office of the Kensington Special Sales Manager. Attn.: Special Sales Department. Kensington Publishing Corp., 119 West 40th Street, New York, NY 10018. Phone: 1-800-221-2647.

Kensington and the K logo Reg. U.S. Pat. & TM Off.

Library of Congress Card Catalogue Number: 2013950843

ISBN-13: 978-0-7582-8503-4
ISBN-10: 0-7582-8503-5
First Kensington Hardcover Edition: January 2014

eISBN-13: 978-0-7582-8505-8
eISBN-10: 0-7582-8505-1
First Kensington Electronic Edition: January 2014

10 9 8 7 6 5 4 3 2 1

Printed in the United States of America

For my brother, Michael, with love

ACKNOWLEDGMENTS

As always, I am enormously grateful to my editor John Scognamiglio for his unwavering faith in Jaine, and to my agent, Evan Marshall, for his ongoing guidance and support.

Thanks to Hiro Kimura, who so brilliantly brings Prozac to life on my book covers. To Lou Malcangi for another eye-catching dust jacket design. And to the rest of the gang at Kensington who keep Jaine and Prozac coming back for murder and minced mackerel guts each year.

Special thanks to Frank Mula, man of a thousand jokes. And to Joanne Fluke, who takes time out from writing her own bestselling Hannah Swensen mysteries to grace me with her insights and friendship—not to mention a cover blurb to die for.

Thanks to Dr. Madelyn Graham, veterinarian extraordinaire. And to Mike O'Toole, whose Gondola Getaway is one of the most fun things you can do in Southern California.

Thanks to John Fluke, product placement guru and all-around great guy. To Mark Baker, who was there from the beginning. And to Jamie Wallace (aka Sidney's mom), the genial webmeister at LauraLevineMysteries.com.

A loving thanks to my friends and family for hanging in with me all these years. And a special shout out to all the readers who've taken the time to write me and/or show up at my book signings. You guys are the best!

And finally, to my most loyal fan and sounding board, my husband Mark. I couldn't do it without you.

Chapter 1

There it was, waiting for me on my bedspread. An early Valentine's gift from my Significant Other.

Gingerly I picked it up.

"A hairball. How very thoughtful."

My cat, Prozac, looked up from where she was lolling on my pillow, beaming with pride.

I left another one for you in your slippers.

At this stage of my life, I was used to crappy Valentine's gifts. Mainly from my ex-husband, The Blob. I remember the Valentine's Day he came sauntering through the door with a slightly wilted bouquet of roses.

"For you, pickleface," he said.

He liked to call me pickleface. One of the many reasons we are no longer married.

The Blob never brought me gifts, not unless you consider a complimentary toothpick from Hop Li's Chinese Restaurant a gift. So my heart actually started to melt just a tad. Seeing a small envelope sticking out from the bouquet, I opened it eagerly, only to read the words:

Rest in peace, Esther.
With heartfelt sympathy, the Rosenkrantzes.

Nothing says Happy Valentine's Day like used funeral flowers.

So like I say, I was used to dreadful Valentine's gifts. But none as dreadful as the one I was about to get that day when Joy Amoroso called.

I was stretched out on my sofa, scraping Prozac's hairball out from my slipper, when the phone rang.

"Jane Eyre?" asked a woman with a decidedly phony British accent.

"Austen," I corrected her. "Jaine Austen."

"Yes, right. Whatever. This is Joy Amoroso calling. You've heard of me, of course."

Something in her tone of voice told me to answer in the affirmative.

"Um, sure," I lied.

"I need someone to write advertising copy, and Marvin Cooper gave me your name."

Marvin Cooper, aka *Marvelous Marv, The Mattress King*, was one of my biggest clients. What a sweetie, I thought, to have recommended me for a job. If I'd only known what hell was in store for me, I would have smothered him with one of his Comfort Cloud pillows. But at that moment, I was thrilled at the prospect of a paycheck winging its way toward my anemic checking account.

"I assume you know all about my business," the phony Brit was saying.

"Of course," I lied again.

"Come to my offices tomorrow at ten a.m., and I'll decide if you're good enough to work for me."

What nerve! I felt like telling her to take her silly job and shove it. She may not have realized it, but she happened to be talking to the woman who won the Golden

Plunger Award from the Los Angeles Plumbers Association for the immortal slogan *In a Rush to Flush? Call Toiletmasters!*

Yes, I would have dearly liked to flip her a verbal finger, but "Okay, sure," were the lily-livered words I actually uttered.

"Good. See you tomorrow. Ten a.m. sharp."

And before even giving me her address, she'd hung up.

Who on earth was this presumptuous woman?

I was just about to head over to my computer to check her out online when there was a knock on my door.

I opened it to find my neighbor, Lance Venable.

A normally bubbly fellow with bright blue eyes and a headful of tight blond curls, Lance looked distinctly bubble-free as he trudged into my apartment.

"Oh, Jaine!" he sighed, summoning his inner Sarah Bernhardt, "I don't think I can face another Valentine's Day without a date." With that, he plopped down on my sofa, his arm slung dramatically across his forehead, very Marcel Proust Yearning for a Madeleine.

"Cheer up, Lance. We'll stay home, order a pizza, and watch *Fatal Attraction* like we always do."

"No, I'm afraid not even the thought of Glenn Close with a butcher knife is going to cheer me up this year. In fact, I was thinking of going to a weekend retreat at a monastery."

"A monastery? But you're not even Catholic."

"That's not the point. I need to meditate, to contemplate, to see how I look in one of those cowl neck robes. And besides, who knows? I just might meet somebody."

"Lance, you can't go to a monastery to pick up guys! They're celibate."

"So? I like a challenge."

The scary thing is, he wasn't kidding.

"But enough about my pathetic life. What's going on in your pathetic life?"

"For your information," I said, scraping the last of Prozac's hairball from my slipper, "my life does not happen to be the least bit pathetic. "But now that you asked, the most maddening thing just happened. I got a phone call from a mystery woman named Joy Amoroso, telling me to come in for a job interview without even giving me her address or the name of her company."

"Joy Amoroso!" Lance's eyes lit up. "I know all about her. She owns Dates of Joy, Beverly Hills's premier matchmaking service!"

He sprang up from the sofa, his lethargy a thing of the past.

"Be right back!" he cried, dashing out the door. Seconds later he was back, as promised, waving a glossy news sheet.

"The Beverly Hills Social Pictorial," he said, leafing through it. "I subscribe to keep track of my customers."

The customers to whom Lance referred were the wealthy dames who shopped at Neiman Marcus's shoe department, where Lance toils as a salesman, fondling billion-dollar bunions for a living.

"Aha!" he cried, finding the page he'd been searching for. "Here she is."

He handed me the magazine, pointing to an ad for the Dates of Joy matchmaking service.

There in the middle of the ad was Joy Amoroso, an attractive blonde sitting behind a desk, a statue of Cupid slinging his arrow in the background. At least, I assumed Joy was attractive. The picture itself was extremely hazy, as if it had been shot through a lens liberally lathered with Vaseline.

"When you get the job," Lance was saying, "you've got to promise you'll get me a date."

"I thought you were going to a monastery."

"A monastery? Why on earth would I go to a monastery when I could be going on a Date of Joy? I hear she's got a client list filled with gazillionaires."

"Don't get your hopes up. I haven't got the job yet."

"Oh, but you will."

And as very bad luck would have it, he was right.

Little did I know it then, but my Valentine's Day was about to go from *Fatal Attraction* to just plain fatal.

Chapter 2

Ifound Beverly Hills's premier matchmaker several miles outside Beverly Hills, in the perfectly pleasant but distinctly less prestigious town of Mar Vista.

Housed in a three-story stucco office building between Ellman's Upholsterers and Jerry's Discount Flowers, Dates of Joy was a far cry from the swellegant mecca of matchmaking I'd imagined.

Nabbing a spot in front of Jerry's Discount Flowers, I made my way past buckets of drooping carnations into Joy's office building. There I stepped onto a musty elevator, where some industrious hoodlums had etched the walls with an impressive display of male genitalia.

I got off at the second floor and found Joy's office at the end of a dank hallway. In contrast to the oatmeal walls surrounding it, Joy's door was painted a bilious Pepto-Bismol pink, the words DATES OF JOY etched in flowery calligraphy.

I headed inside to find the walls painted the same Pepto-Bismol pink and lined with large framed blowups of happy couples gazing at each other, gooey-eyed with love.

At the time, I assumed that they were all Joy's satisfied customers.

Seated at a receptionist's desk was a goth pixie clad in

black leather and a tasteful assortment of body piercings, her spiky hair a blazing shade of purple. And hunched over a computer behind her was a skinny guy in black horn-rimmed glasses held together at the hinges with duct tape. In his white short-sleeved shirt and yellow bow tie, cowlicks running riot in his hair, the guy had Computer Nerd written all over him.

"May I help you?" the goth pixie asked, looking up from her computer, a steel stud glinting merrily in her nose.

"I'm Jaine Austen. I'm here to see Joy Amoroso."

"Oh, right."

Was it my imagination, or was that a look of pity I'd just seen flit across her face?

"Joy will be right with you," she said. "Won't you have a seat?"

She gestured to a row of plastic chairs lined up against the wall. I plopped down into one and checked out the reading matter on a tiny coffee table in front of me. Along with the usual dog-eared issues of *People* was a thick loose-leaf binder.

"That's our Date Book, with pictures of our clients," said the pixie, whose name, according to the ID bracelet tattooed on her wrist, was Cassie.

I opened the book, expecting to find a bunch of bald heads and stomach paunches, but the book was stuffed with stunners. One good looking prospect after the next. Joy certainly had a lot of hotties on tap.

Just as I was ogling a particularly adorable tousle-haired studmuffin, the door to Joy's office opened and out walked the date-meister herself.

The woman in front of me bore little resemblance to the photo in her ad. That picture had been taken at least ten years and fifty pounds ago. Joy Amoroso was still an attractive woman with deceptively angelic features. Button nose, big blue eyes, and a fabulous head of streaked blond hair. But that pretty face of hers came with an impressive set of chins, and she was clearly packing quite a few pounds under her flowy A-line dress. Only her feet were tiny—slender little things encased in what looked like nosebleed expensive designer shoes.

"Jaine!" she cried with the same phony British accent she'd used on the phone. "So teddibly sorry to keep you waiting."

She looked me up and down with all the subtlety of a New York City construction worker. I guess I must have passed muster, because she then asked: "Won't you step into my office, hon?"

Tearing myself away from my tousle-haired dreamboat, I grabbed my book of writing samples and followed her into her inner sanctum.

Like the reception area, Joy's office was filled with framed photos of happy couples. But unlike the no-frills furniture in the reception area, Joy's decor ran to the antique and ornate. A Marie Antoinette-ish desk and chair dominated the room, along with an étagère crammed with fussy knickknacks. Over in a corner lurked the same statue of Cupid I'd seen in Joy's ad, now shooting his arrow up at what looked like a water stain on the ceiling.

But what caught my eye most of all was an open box of Godiva chocolates on Joy's desk, chock full of creamy dark chocolate truffles.

My taste buds, napping after the cinnamon raisin bagel I'd had for breakfast, suddenly jolted awake. A truffle sure would've hit the spot right about then. Of course, a truffle would hit the spot with me just about any time. But those velvety Godivas looked particularly mouthwatering.

Taking a seat behind her desk, Joy popped one in her

mouth. My taste buds and I waited for her to offer me one, but alas, we waited in vain.

Obviously Joy was not a sharer.

She gestured for me to sit in one of the froufrou chairs facing her desk, and as I did, I felt a broken spring poke me in the fanny.

"Comfy?" she asked.

"Very," I lied, still hoping for one of those Godivas.

"So," she said, sucking chocolate from her fingertips, "Marvin Cooper tells me you're a wonderful writer."

I blushed modestly.

"But I'll be the judge of that," she added with a grim smile.

She held out her hand for my sample book. I only hoped she didn't smear chocolate all over my Toiletmasters campaign.

As she leafed through my ads, I whiled away the minutes looking at pictures of the happy couples on the wall and trying to ignore the spring poking me in my fanny.

"Not bad," she said when she was finally through.

Then she got up and began pacing the room in her teeny designer-clad tootsies, launching into what had all the earmarks of a well-rehearsed campaign speech.

"As you well know," she began, "Dates of Joy is the preeminent dating service in Beverly Hills."

I wisely refrained from pointing out that we were a good three and a half miles from Beverly Hills.

"I handle only the crème de la crème of the L.A. dating scene. Movers and shakers. And all sorts of celebrities. My fees start at ten thousand dollars a year. And go up. Way up."

Wow. And I thought my Fudge of the Month Club was expensive.

"And I'm worth it," she said, her chins quivering with pride. "I'm the best there is. That's because I've got matchmaking in my blood. My mother was a match-maker, and her mother before her."

Not only that, according to Joy, one of her royal ancestors back in jolly old England was the one who fixed up Anne Boleyn with Henry VIII.

I nodded as if I actually believed her.

If this woman was English royalty, I was a Tibetan monk.

"Although I abhor the idea of self promotion," she was saying, "I have to keep up with the times. So I'm looking for someone to write copy for a sales brochure. "So whaddaya think?" she asked, dumping her royal accent. "You interested?"

"Sounds very intriguing."

Time to see how much gold was at the end of this particular rainbow.

"And the pay?" I asked.

"I was thinking somewhere in the neighborhood of three grand."

Someone call the movers! That's my kind of neighborhood.

And yet, a little voice inside me was telling me to run for the hills. I knew trouble when I saw it coming down the pike, and I could tell Joy Amoroso was trouble with a capital OMG! That bossy manner, that insane Queen Mum accent that seemed to come and go like an over-booked call girl on New Year's Eve. The woman would drive me up a wall in no time.

Why not save myself the aggravation and just say no?

So what if I owed a few bucks to MasterCard? And Macy's? And the Fudge of the Month Club? So what if the Fudge of the Month Club cut off my membership and I never got another box of fudge ever again—not even the white chocolate macadamia nut fudge I'm particularly fond of?

Surely I could live without white chocolate macadamia nut fudge.

Couldn't I?

Oh, please. We all know the answer to that one.

"So," Joy asked, popping another chocolate in her mouth. "Is it a deal?"

"It's a deal."

And that, in a macadamia nutshell, was how I came to sell my soul to the Matchmaker from Hell.

"You'll start tomorrow at nine," Joy commanded. "I want you to hang out at the office for a few days to get the picture of how I work."

I'd get the picture, all right.

And trust me, it was not a pretty one.

Riding up the elevator in Joy's office building the next morning, I found myself elbow to elbow with a gal who looked like she just stepped out of a Victoria's Secret catalog. Pouty lips. Eensy waist. And boobs that made it onto the elevator a good thirty seconds before she did. Surely she wasn't going to see Joy. A woman like that needed help finding a date like I needed help finding the cookie aisle in the supermarket.

But much to my surprise, when she got out of the elevator, she trotted straight to Joy's Pepto-Bismol door.

I followed her inside and blinked in surprise to see the reception area was crammed with stunning guys and gals.

"I'm here for the casting session," Ms. Secret told Cassie, who was seated at her desk, a skull and crossbones barrette adorning her bright purple hair.

A casting session, huh? I figured Joy was looking for models to use in her new brochure.

"Take a seat in the photo studio," Cassie told Ms. Secret, pointing to a large room adjacent to the reception area. I peeked inside and saw about a dozen other Beautiful People sitting around, chatting among themselves and gazing at their own head shots with unabashed admiration.

"Hi, Jaine," Cassie said, catching sight of me. "Joy will be tied up for a while. Until she's free, she wants you to work with Travis."

She pointed to the bow-tied geek I'd noticed yesterday.

"I'm supposed to show you our Web site," he said, pulling up a chair for me next to his computer.

"So what's going on?" I asked with a nod to the beautiful people. "Is Joy casting models for the brochure?"

"Not exactly."

He glanced at Joy's door, as if to make sure she wasn't listening.

"Remember the date book you saw yesterday? With pictures of Joy's clients? Well, hardly any of the people in that book are actual clients. Most of them are models or actors. Every once in a while Joy holds a phony casting session, pretending she's going to shoot a TV commercial. All the models and actors leave their headshots, and then Joy puts them into her date book."

"No way!"

"That's how she reels in the new clients," he nodded.

"What about all her movers and shakers? And her celebrity clients?"

Cassie, who had been listening in, now turned around, guffawing. "Are you kidding? The closest we ever got to a celebrity was when Reese Witherspoon's maid came looking for Ellman's Upholsterers next door."

"My job is to scan the headshots and put them on the Web site," Travis explained. "And Joy wants you to write phony bios to go along with the pictures."

"Phony bios? She never told me about that yesterday."

"There's lots of things Joy never tells you," Travis said with a bitter laugh. "Like how she expects you to pick up her dry cleaning on weekends."

"Or get her Thai food at one in the morning," Cassie chimed in.

I bristled in annoyance.

If Joy thought I was going to compromise my integrity by writing phony bios to lure in unsuspecting clients, she had another think coming. We Austens have our principles. I'd simply tell her it was no dice.

But then I remembered the stack of unpaid bills multiplying like rabbits on my dining room table.

Oh, well. What harm could it do to write a few teensy bios? After all, surely Joy had some legitimate clients, people whose lives she actually improved.

"So where are Joy's actual clients?" I asked.

"Here they are," Travis said, clicking open another file.

Suddenly his computer screen was filled with real human beings, people with thinning hair and thick waists, with noses and breasts that had never seen a surgeon's knife. All of them smiling into the camera with a look of hopeful desperation in their eyes.

Travis was scrolling from one photo to the next when he stopped at a photo of a truly lovely woman. A fragile wisp of a thing with startling blue eyes and a nimbus of silken blond hair framing a perfectly chiseled Grace Kelly face.

"Who's she?" I asked, assuming she was a model mistakenly stuck in the Real People file.

"She used to be a client," Travis said.

"What a beauty."

"She sure was," Cassie echoed, swiveling around in her chair and staring down at Travis's computer screen.

"She dropped out of the club years ago," Travis said. "But Joy keeps her photo on the site to lure in the new clients."

We continued scrolling through real clients, uncovering some genuinely attractive daters here and there, but they were few and far between.

Meanwhile, the model/actors continued to stream in and out of Joy's office, leaving their head shots with Cassie.

"Ta ta!" Joy would trill in her phony British accent as each hopeful left. "I'll let your agent know as soon as I make up my mind."

"As if that's ever going to happen," Travis muttered.

"I don't suppose Joy's really British?" I asked after one particularly hammy "Ta ta!"

Travis and Cassie had a hearty chuckle over that one.

"Are you kidding?" Cassie smirked. "Her real name is Joy Woznowski. And she was born in the Bronx. Which I know for a fact because I've snooped at her passport."

Having exposed Joy for the utter phony she was, Cassie swiveled back to her desk, while Travis and I returned to the Web site. Travis was pointing out which bios Joy wanted me to write when suddenly what seemed like a minor hurricane erupted from Joy's office.

Joy came storming out into the middle of the reception area, tottering on her tiny heels, her face purple with rage.

"Who ate my chocolate?" she screeched, holding out her box of Godivas.

The remaining models looked at each other, unnerved.

"One of them is missing!" Joy stomped around the room, shoving the box under everyone's nose. The models. Cassie. Travis. And moi, her gaze lingering for an uncomfortable beat on my thighs.

"Which one of you took it? Huh? Huh? Huh?"

At this point one of the models, a skittish young thing in leather pants and a tank top, grabbed his portfolio and scooted out the door.

"If I find out you did it, you'll be in big trouble!" Joy shouted out after him.

"There were six chocolates in the box," she said, turning back to the rest of us. "And now there are only five! See?"

She started counting out the chocolates in the box.

"One . . . two . . . three . . . four . . . five . . ."

Then she looked down and saw what we all saw: The sixth chocolate.

You'd think she would have been embarrassed. But no. Hurricane Joy, having spent all her venom, just shrugged and said, "Never mind."

As she tottered back into her office, the models broke out in a chorus of nervous whispers. But Travis and Cassie just rolled their eyes.

"This happens all the time," Cassie said with a shrug.

Holy mackerel. And I thought *I* was a chocoholic.

I trudged up the path to my duplex in the slums of Beverly Hills, a modest pocket of no-frills dwellings far from the mega-mansions north of Wilshire Boulevard. I was still shuddering at the memory of Hurricane Joy when Lance came bounding out from his apartment.

"So did you get the job?" he asked, his eyes lighting up at the sight of me.

"Yeah, I got it," I sighed.

"Great!" he beamed, ignoring the cloud of gloom

hovering over my head. "Now you can have Joy fix me up on a date."

"Forget it, Lance. The woman is a crook. She pads her client list with models and actors who don't even belong to the club. Most of the guys who do belong are a lot older and paunchier than you. I saw a grand total of five attractive male clients on her active client list, only one of whom was gay. And he lived in Rancho Cucamonga with six cats and a Maserati."

"A Maserati, huh? Works for me! So set me up with an appointment ASAP."

"I'm not setting you up with an appointment. Joy's fees start at ten grand a year, and there's no way you can afford that."

"We'll see about that."

And with a sly look, a lot like Prozac's just before she's about to pounce on a cashmere sweater, he trotted off into the night.

Back in my apartment, I checked my messages, praying that an assignment had come in from one of my regular clients. Eagerly I scanned my e-mails for a note from Toiletmasters (*Flushed with Success Since 1995!*) or Tip Top Cleaners (*We Clean for You. We Press for You. We Even Dye for You!*) or Ackerman's Awnings (*Just a Shade Better*). But alas, my in-box was depressingly devoid of job orders.

For the time being, it looked like I was stuck with the Godiva Godzilla.

YOU'VE GOT MAIL!

To: Jausten
From: Shoptillyoudrop
Subject: Exciting News!

Exciting news, honey! I just ordered the most adorable Georgie O. Armani jacket from the shopping channel. Lipstick red with white piping. It'll be perfect for Valentine's Day. Daddy is taking me to dinner at Le Chateaubriand, Tampa Vistas's most elegant restaurant. Daddy promised he'd make the reservations today. He's probably getting me what he always gets me for Valentine's Day: a dozen roses and a bottle of Jean Naté. I'm getting him something he saw on an infomercial, some crazy gadget called a Belgian Army Knife. I wanted to buy him a watch from the shopping channel, but no, he had to have that silly Belgian Army Knife. He insists he can't live without it.

But enough about Daddy. Here's the really exciting news. Guess who's moved to Tampa Vistas. Lydia Pinkus's brother, Lester. You remember Lydia Pinkus, don't you, honey? One of my dearest friends and the president of the Tampa Vistas Homeowners Association. Anyhow, her brother is the most charming man, a retired physics pro-fessor, a world traveler, and a former amateur boxer. And so distinguished. He looks just like the doctor on the Lipitor commercials!

He's staying with Lydia until he can find a townhouse of his own. And today he's taking me and Lydia and Edna Lindstrom to lunch at the clubhouse. Isn't that the sweetest thing ever?

Must run and get dressed.

Love and XXX,
Mom

To: Jausten
From: DaddyO
Subject: Horrible News!

Horrible news, Lambchop. Lydia Pinkus's brother, a retired physics professor, has moved to Tampa Vistas. What an insufferable gasbag. Yapping about black holes and antiquarks and bragging about how he used to be an amateur boxer. Big deal. I used to be on the varsity Ping-Pong team in college, but you don't catch me bragging about it.

It's bad enough having to put up with that battle axe Lydia. Now I have to put up with her gasbag brother, too. He's taking your mom and Edna Lindstrom to lunch at the clubhouse today. Thank God I don't have to go, too. If I had to hear one more story about quantum chromodynamics or the time Lester sparred with Sugar Ray Leonard, I swear I'd conk out head first in my chicken noodle soup.

But on the plus side, Lambchop, your mom is getting me a fantastic gift for Valentine's Day. A genuine Belgian Army Knife. It's just like a Swiss Army knife, only it comes with a built-in callus remover—and a free recipe for Belgian waffles!

More later. Gotta call and make reservations for

Valentine's dinner at Le Chateaubriand. It's Tampa Vistas's most exclusive restaurant, you know.

Love 'n' hugs from,
Daddy

P.S. I think Lester Pinkus has a "thing" for your mom. I've caught him staring at her when he thought I wasn't looking.

**To: Jausten
From: Shoptillyoudrop
Subject: Silliest Thing You Ever Heard**

Forgot to tell you, sweetheart. Daddy thinks Lester Pinkus has a crush on me. Isn't that the silliest thing you ever heard?

XOXO,
Mom

**To: Jausten
From: DaddyO
Subject: Gasbag Romeo**

Unsettling news, Lambchop. I just happened to be walking by the clubhouse restaurant a while ago, and you'll never guess what I saw! Lester Pinkus holding hands with your mom! What did I tell you? I knew that gasbag Romeo was up to no good!

Love 'n' snuggles from
Your very irate,
Daddy

To: Jausten
From: Shoptillyoudrop
Subject: The Death of Me Yet

I swear, honey, your father will be the death of me yet. He
thinks Lester Pinkus and I were holding hands in the
clubhouse dining room! Of all the absurd ideas! It turns
out Lester studied palm reading in Nepal (such a multi-
talented man!) and was giving us all palm readings. He
told Edna she had an extra-long life line, and saw
wonderful things in her future. She was so excited, she
almost forgot to go back for seconds at the buffet.
Anyhow, just as it was my turn to get my palm read,
Daddy showed up. He claims he just happened to be
walking by. Oh, puh-leese. I know your Daddy, and he
was spying on us! Now he thinks Lester Pinkus was holding my hand!

I can't write any more now, darling. I'm way too upset.

Yours, desperately in need of Oreos—
Mom

To: Jausten
From: DaddyO
Subject: Sadly Mistaken

If Lester Pinkus thinks he can woo your mother away from
me, he's sadly mistaken. I still haven't gotten around to
making those reservations at Le Chateaubriand, but when
I do, I'm going to get the best table in the house and show
your mom what a true Romeo is made of.

XXX,
Daddy

P.S. Did I tell you my Belgian Army Knife comes with built-
in nose hair trimmers? Cool, huh?

Chapter 3

The Case of the Missing Godiva was just a taste of things to come. Life with Joy, as I was about to discover, was one constant hissy fit.

Over the next few days I watched in dismay as she ran roughshod over her staff, screeching at Cassie for not answering the phone fast enough and bringing her Sweet'n Low instead of Splenda for her coffee. Afraid of identity theft, she was constantly changing her AOL password, and then screaming at Travis when she couldn't remember it.

But the minute a client walked through the door, she was sweet as pie, Mother Teresa in Manolos.

My second day on the job, I got to see her in action with a new client.

I was in Joy's office, listening to her ramble on about her matchmaking triumphs and, not incidentally, thinking about the e-mails I'd received from my parents that morning.

For those of you who haven't already met them, you should know that my parents are disaster magnets of the highest order. Wherever they go, catastrophe seems to follow. Although Mom, a confirmed TV shopaholic, is not without her quirks, Daddy is the family's designated crazymaker. I swear, he can take an ordinary day and turn it into a headline on the evening news. Poor Mom deserves a Congressional Medal of Honor for putting up with him all these years. I sincerely doubted Lester Pinkus had a crush on Mom. Just another case of Daddy's imagination running wild.

I was sitting there, hoping Daddy would come to his senses without too much collateral damage, when Cassie poked her head in the door.

"Someone to see you, Joy. He says he's interested in joining the club."

Immediately Joy morphed into Queen Mum mode.

"How teddibly nice to meet you," she said as Cassie ushered in a short, pasty-faced gnome of a guy, all spiffed up in brown shoes, white socks, and his Sunday best pocket protector.

His name, embroidered on his company work shirt, was Barry.

Joy sat him down in one of her fussy Marie Antoinette chairs.

"So how can I help you . . . Barry?" she asked, reading his name off his chest.

Barry smiled shyly, revealing a most disconcerting gap between his two front teeth, then launched into a heartrending tale of his non-existent love life.

"I haven't had a date since high school," he confessed, "when my mother made me take my cousin to the senior prom."

"You poor darling," Joy tsked, fake empathy oozing from every pore.

"I've tried all the online dating services, and never got chosen once, except by a woman named Brandy, who said she charged a hundred dollars an hour. But for me, two hundred."

"Why, that's disgraceful!" The Queen Mum was outraged. "These online dating services are nothing but a waste of money. You don't want a silly computer trying to find you a date. You need the personalized services of an expert matchmaker." At which point she launched into her spiel about coming from a long line of match-makers dating back to Charlemagne. (When last I'd heard that whopper, it was Henry VIII. Somehow she'd managed to add a few extra limbs to her family tree.)

Barry sat there with his mouth open, entranced by her every word.

"When you sign up with Dates of Joy, I personally hand pick the woman of your dreams."

"Gosh," he said, eyes wide with wonder.

"Here. Let me show you some of your potential dates."

And then she laid it on him. The coup de grâce. The Date Book. Larded with photos of unavailable models and actresses.

He blinked in amazement as she turned the pages.

"These girls are members of your club?"

"Absolutely," Joy lied, smooth as velvet.

"But they'd never go out with someone like me."

So Barry was not quite as clueless as he looked.

"Oh, you'd be surprised," Joy said. "So many of my lady clients are fed up with the shallow men they meet here in Los Angeles. They don't care about superficial things like looks and income. They're searching for deeper qualities in a man, like warmth and sensitivity, qualities I sense you possess in spades."

"Ya think?" Barry asked, scratching some wax out of his ear.

"Absolutely!"

"Okay, I want Albany!" Barry pointed at a picture of a spectacular redhead, the kind of vixen you see tossing her hair in a shampoo commercial. "When can I go out with her?"

"Soon, very soon," Joy assured him. "But first," she added, flashing him a deceptively angelic smile, "there's a little matter of finances. Here at Dates of Joy, our fees start at ten thousand dollars a year."

"Ten thousand dollars?" He gulped.

"It's normally twenty-five thousand, but I'm giving you a discounted rate because I sense you're a quality person."

If she told one more lie, she'd turn into a congressman.

Poor Barry's face blanched at the news of Joy's outrageous fees, and I breathed a sigh of relief. Surely it would be a matter of milliseconds before he was bounding out the door and hurrying back to the friendly folks at Match.com.

But no, much to my consternation, he scratched some more wax out of his ear, musing, "I have a ten-thousand-dollar CD that's coming due. It's my entire life savings. I was going to roll it over, but maybe I could cash it in."

"Don't!" I wanted to cry.

"You won't regret it," Joy said, giving Satan a run for his money in the dirty tricks department.

"I guess I'll just run over to the bank and get the money."

"Why go to all the bother?" Joy cooed. "Just call them up and transfer the money to your checking account, and you can write me a check here and now."

I could see the wheels in her devious little brain spinning. She was not about to take a chance that he'd walk out the door and change his mind on his way to the bank.

And like a dope, Barry got on the phone and closed down his CD, giving the banker at the other end of the line his Social Security number and mother's maiden name, all of which I feared Joy was memorizing for future use.

Minutes later he was writing Joy a check for ten grand.

Tucking his check in her bosom, Joy ushered Barry out of her office with a royal "ta ta," assuring him he'd soon be tripping the light fantastic with the woman of his dreams.

"Where the hell am I ever going to find a woman desperate enough to go out with that bozo?" she muttered the minute he was gone.

As I listened to him out in the reception area setting up an appointment with Cassie to have his picture taken for the date book, I was overcome by a sense of dread. This poor man was about to step in a bog of fiscal quicksand, and I was just sitting there doing nothing. I couldn't let him go through with it!

When I heard him leave the office, I jumped up from my chair.

"Excuse me," I said to Joy, who was treating herself to a Godiva. "Be right back. I've got to use the ladies' room."

Without waiting for a reply, I scooted out of the office and went racing down the corridor. Thank heavens Barry was still there, waiting for the elevator.

"Barry!" I called out.

"Yes?" He turned to look at me, beaming, no doubt, at the thought of his future date with Albany.

"If you know what's good for you," I whispered, "you'll stop payment on your check."

He blinked in confusion.

"Why would I do that?"

I wanted to tell him the truth, that Joy was a lying, cheating, amoral chocoholic whose date book was a total sham. But I had to be careful. The last thing I wanted was a slander lawsuit on my hands.

"Let's just say it might not work out as well as you think," I offered lamely.

"Don't be silly. Joy said I'd meet the woman of my dreams. And Joy would never let me down. She's great."

"Really," I called after him as he stepped in the elevator. "Give it some thought."

Poor innocent lamb, I thought as the elevator door closed and he began his descent. Little did he know how far he was about to fall.

I hurried back to Joy's office, where I found her chomping down on another Godiva.

I wondered what she'd do if I reached over and plucked one from the box.

Scenes from *Apocalypse Now* immediately sprang to mind.

Instead I took some Tic Tacs from my purse.

"Care for a Tic Tac?" I asked pointedly, hoping she'd get the message that sharing was a Good Thing.

"Yuck, no," she replied, totally oblivious, and picked up where she'd left off on her ramble about her lifetime achievements.

I took out my steno pad and took desultory notes, inwardly rolling my eyes at each outrageous bit of puffery. She actually expected me to believe that she had fixed up Nelson Mandela on one of his first dates out of prison.

She was in the middle of one such colossal whopper when the door to her office opened and in walked a raven-haired hunk in tight leather pants and a silk shirt unbuttoned practically to his navel. Six-pack abs waxed to perfection peeked out from the deep V in his shirt.

All very Rodeo Drive Hit Man.

Joy's eyes lit up at the sight of him.

"Tonio, honey!" she cried.

"Hey, babe," he said, sauntering in, giving me an up close and personal look at his impressive tush.

If those leather pants of his were any tighter, they'd be a tourniquet.

"Who's this?" he asked, raking me over with bedroom eyes that came complete with satin sheets and an overhead mirror.

"This is Jaine Austen," Joy said. "The writer I told you about. Jaine, this is my boyfriend, Tonio."

"Nice to meetcha," Tonio said, then slithered over to Joy and, totally unabashed by my presence, bent down and planted a wet smacker on her lips.

"Miss me, babe?"

She nodded mutely, her eyes glazed over with lust.

Okay, class. Time out for discussion. What, we must ask ourselves, is wrong with this picture? What was a serious hottie like Tonio doing with the Godiva Godzilla?

I was about to find out.

"Hey, babe," he said. "I just saw a great shirt over at Barneys, but I'm a little short on cash. Can you spot me two hundred?"

The glow in Joy's eyes dimmed just a tad.

"Can't you use your credit card?"

"Those idiots at Visa cut me off," Tonio said with a careless shrug. "It's some kinda clerical error. I'll have it sorted out in no time."

Joy bristled in annoyance, but then Tonio bent down and nuzzled her neck. Instantly her eyes went all soft and gooey.

With a sigh, she reached for her purse and pulled out an impressive wad of dough.

"Here," she said, peeling off two hundred-dollar bills.

"Thanks, babe."

Then, with a wave and a wink, Tonio was out the door.

Whaddaya know?

Looked like somebody had a boy toy. And an expensive one at that.

Chapter 4

"Jaine!" Joy was beaming at me when I showed up at her office the next day. "I've got the most marvelous news, and you'll never guess what it is."

"You've decided to go straight and turn yourself in to the Better Business Bureau?"

Okay, I didn't really say that.

"In order for you to get a better idea of how my service works," Joy announced, "I'm going to treat you to your very own Date of Joy!"

"How nice," I murmured.

I only hoped it wasn't with Barry, aka Mr. Pocket Protector.

"But first you're going to need a makeover. I can't possibly have your picture in my date book with that godawful haircut."

Well! Of all the nerve.

(Fatima at Supercuts, if you're reading this, my deepest apologies.)

"Cassie!" she shrieked, summoning her purple-haired aide-de-camp. "Drop what you're doing and give Jaine a complete makeover. Haircut and makeup. The works!"

Cassie gathered some supplies and took me to the ladies' room across the hall to wash my hair.

"Isn't this a public health violation?" I asked as

Cassie worked up a lather with a lovely citrus-scented shampoo.

"Of course it is," Cassie blithely replied. "But Joy thinks she can get away with anything. And you know what? Somehow she always does."

After my shampoo, Cassie led me back to Joy's photo studio, where she sat me down in a director's chair and began snipping away at my curly locks.

I must confess I was a tad nervous getting a haircut from a woman with purple hair and a nose ring. But much to my surprise, she did a pretty fantastic job.

When left untamed, my hair bears a striking resemblance to Shirley Temple's on the Good Ship Lollipop. Very Curls Gone Wild. Usually I spend ages trying to tame them into submission, but Cassie let them sprong to their hearts' content, shaping them to perfection, giving me the kind of sophisticated do you rarely see at Supercuts.

(Oops. Sorry, Fatima.)

She showed equal skill with her makeup supplies, dabbing on this and brushing on that. When she was through, my eyes looked larger, my skin clearer, and best of all, I had actual cheekbones! Wow, if I lost a few gazillion pounds, I could practically be a stunt double for Sarah Jessica Parker!

"You're so good at this, Cassie!" I said, unable to tear myself away from my reflection in the mirror.

"Thanks," she said with a shy smile.

Eventually Cassie managed to wrench me from the mirror and trotted me into Joy's office for inspection.

"What do you think?" Cassie asked, spinning me around.

"Fabulous!" Joy exclaimed. "Just fabulous!"

"Thanks, Joy. I really appreciate this."

"It's nothing," Joy replied. "I'll just deduct three hundred dollars from your paycheck."

She was charging me? For a makeover I didn't even ask for? What monumental chutzpah!

And speaking of chutzpah, we were about to get another dose when Travis poked his head in the door and announced, "Jaine, there's someone here to see you."

At which point Lance Venable, the Chutzpah King himself, came sailing into the room, all duded up in a designer suit, his blond curls moussed to perfection. And if I wasn't mistaken, it looked like he'd popped in for a quick trip to the tanning salon.

"Jaine, honeybun!" he cried, affecting the most god-awful Southern accent. "How mawvelous you look!"

"Cassie just gave me a makeover," I said.

"A little gift from me to Jaine," Joy had the gall to say.

Then she turned to Cassie and Travis and dismissed them with an impatient wave.

"Jaine, darlin'," Lance drawled, still doing his Southern accent. "Ah'm afraid ah'm a wee bit early for owah lunch date."

Needless to say, we had no lunch date. And I will not bother trying to replicate his idiotic accent beyond this point. It was bad enough having to listen to it in the first place.

"Why, I do declare!" he cried, turning to Joy. "You must be Joy Amoroso, Matchmaker Extraordinaire. I've heard so many wonderful things about you!"

Joy preened and quickly segued into Queen Mum mode.

"How teddibly kind of you."

Between the two of them, I felt like I was at the Boris & Natasha Royal Academy of Bad Accents.

"I thought you were pretty in your photos," Lance was saying, "but you're even lovelier in person."

He stood back and looked at her, clasping his hands in admiration. "That hair! Those eyes! Anyone ever tell you, you bear a striking resemblance to Scarlett Johansson?"

My God, if he laid it on any thicker, he'd need a trowel. Could she possibly be buying any of this?

Apparently yes.

Because the next thing I knew, she was reaching for her treasured Godiva box and saying, "Care for a chocolate?"

"I really shouldn't," he said with a wink, "but when it comes to Godiva, I simply can't resist."

He plucked one from the box and took a dainty bite.

"Jaine's told me such wonderful things about your fabulous service," he said, "I've decided to give it a try."

"Have a seat," Joy said, gesturing to one of her rump-sprung chairs, "and tell me all about yourself."

"To start," Lance said, with a ridiculous little bow, "my name is Lance Vanderbilt Venable."

Vanderbilt?? Since when?

Joy perked up, interested. "Vanderbilt? Any relation to Cornelius?"

"A wee bit, on Mumsie's side."

Oh, puhleese.

By now Joy was ready to dandle him on her knee and hand-feed him chocolates straight from the box.

"So where have you been all my life, Mr. Venable?" she crooned.

I tactfully refrained from pointing out that for half of it, he wasn't even born.

Lance sat back in his chair and let the lies flow like lava.

"I grew up on our estate in Virginia, dabbled a little at the Sorbonne, came home to work on one of our oil wells, and then thought it would be a kick to move out to Los Angeles."

Wait, I felt like saying. *You left out your stint as advisor to the Pope.*

"Right now I'm head shoe buyer at Neiman Marcus," he said, giving himself a hefty promotion. "I've always wanted to work in fashion, and I'm having the time of my life. It turns out I just adore women and their shoes.

"Love yours, by the way," he added. "Louboutins, aren't they?"

She nodded.

"You have amazing taste."

"I do, don't I?" she preened.

By now they'd totally forgotten about me, and I stood there about as important a player in this scene as the statue of Cupid in the corner.

"And just why," Joy asked, "would a young man of your obvious appeal need my services?"

"Oh, it's easy for me to meet men," Lance said. "But all too often I've discovered"—here he paused for a dramatic batting of the eyes—"all they're interested in is my name and my money. I want to meet a quality man who'll love me for myself."

With Herculean effort, he managed to work up a runt of a teardrop, which he wiped away with a dramatic flourish.

Joy reached across the desk and took his hands in hers, no doubt getting chocolate all over them.

"You poor darling," she clucked. "Fortunately I happen to have a small but very exclusive gay clientele, and I think I know just the man for you! Donny Johnson! Wonderful fellow. I'm not supposed to say anything, but just between you and me"—they still had no I idea I was standing there—"rumor has it Donny's family are the Johnsons of Johnson & Johnson."

I believed that one about as much as I believed Lance was a Vanderbilt.

"Sounds divine!" Lance gushed. "Doesn't it, Jaine?"

At last, someone remembered I was alive.

"Yep, just divine."

I smiled serenely, waiting to see how he was going to cough up the necessary cash to cross the finish line.

Joy now released his hand and segued into Business Mode.

"Membership fees start at fifty thousand dollars," Joy blithely lied. "But because I'm so very fond of you, Lance, I'll make it twenty-five. How would you care to pay? Cash? Check? Credit card? Stock options?"

"Oh." Lance pursed his lips in a tiny moue of concern. "I'm afraid I don't have that kind of money available right now. All my assets are tied up in a pesky trust fund."

Joy's smile was rapidly fading.

"But I should be getting it at the end of next month," he assured her.

"Why don't we wait until then," Joy said, sliding the cover back on her Godiva box, "before we get started?"

Aha! I knew she wouldn't buy it!

But I'd underestimated Lance. Just when I thought the game was over, he struck back.

"Oh, foo. I was so looking forward to getting started. I guess I'll just have to sign up with Carson Hendrick over at the Billionaire Boys Club. He's been positively hounding me to join."

"Carson Hendrick?" Joy scoffed. "That hack?"

I could see Lance had got her where he wanted her. Joy was torn. On the one hand, she could sign him up now and risk getting stiffed, or she could let him go and risk seeing a competitor get all his dough.

And that's when Lance went in for the kill.

"I've got an idea," he said. "Until my inheritance comes through, I'll get you all the designer shoes you want with my Neiman Marcus thirty percent employee discount."

"Thirty percent, huh?"

"It can go up as high as eighty percent during special sales events."

That did it. She was hooked.

"Welcome, darling Lance," she said, throwing out her arms, "to Dates of Joy! Normally I'd have Travis take your picture for our date book, but I know Donny's going to love you. Leave your contact information with Cassie at the front desk, and I'll have him call you."

"Super!" Lance said, leaping up. "Can't wait to meet him. In the meanwhile, is it all right if I steal Jaine away for lunch? I promised I'd take her for a bite at the Jonathan Club."

"Of course, hon. Anything you say. Ta ta, darlings."

She dismissed us with her Queen Mum wave, and Lance herded me out the door, but not before swiping another chocolate from Joy's Godiva box.

"You don't mind, do you, darlin'?" he cooed.

No doubt about it. It looked like Joy had at last met her match in the Monumental Chutzpah Department.

Chapter 5

The Jonathan Club happens to be one of the most exclusive joints in L.A., where the one percent meet to steer clear of the rest of us 99ers.

Needless to say, Lance did not take me there for lunch.

Instead he opted for the slightly less prestigious Der Wienerschnitzel, where we dined al fresco on chili cheese dogs and fries, taking in the scenic view of the gas station across the alley.

Of course, Lance would spend at least 347 hours at his gym burning off Der Wienerschnitzel's industrial-strength calories. I, on the other hand, have a "live and let live" policy where calories are concerned, and planned to let them settle merrily alongside the others nestled on my thighs.

"Why, I do declayah!" Lance said, after tucking into his chow. "This wiener is divine!"

"Enough with the accent, Lance. Any minute now you'll be calling for your mammy and putting on your gown for the barbecue at Twelve Oaks."

"I've always pictured myself a modern day Ashley Wilkes," Lance drawled, a faraway look in his eyes. "Brooding, sensitive, and secretly in love with Big Sam."

"Do you actually plan to keep talking like this on your date with Donny Johnson?"

"Sho 'nuff."

"And by the way, I sincerely doubt Donny's an heir to the Johnson & Johnson fortune. Joy's almost as big a faker as you are. You'll be lucky if he can afford to pick up the check at Der Wienerschnitzel."

"Oh, don't be such a buzz kill," Lance pouted. "It's possible Donny might be filthy rich and insanely handsome."

"Dream on," I said, inhaling the last of my chili cheese dog.

Boy, that sure went down fast, didn't it?

"So what's with the makeover?" Lance eyed my new haircut. "You look great."

"Thanks. You're not the only one going on a Date of Joy. Joy's fixing me up with somebody, too."

Lance's eyes lit up.

"That's wonderful, Jaine! I bet this time you're going to meet your prince charming!"

Then his brow furrowed with concern.

"But whatever you do, promise me you won't wear elastic waist pants on your date."

For some reason, Lance is convinced I've got no fashion sense. He says moths come to my closet to commit suicide. Which is perfectly absurd, as anyone who's ever seen my vintage collection of CUCKOO FOR COCOA PUFFS T-shirts will be the first to tell you.

"Did you hear me, Jaine?" Lance was waving a fry in my face. "No elastic waist pants."

"But I like elastic waist pants. They're so comfortable."

"So are granny nightgowns. But you wouldn't wear one on a date, would you . . . ? Well? Would you?"

"I'm thinking, I'm thinking. With the right elastic waist pants, it might not look so bad."

"No more fries." He slapped my hand away from his plate. (I'd long since finished my own and had started filching his.) "Unless you promise. No elastic waists."

"Oh, all right," I sighed. "No elastic waists."

Having overturned the lone obstacle to my finding true love, Lance resumed waxing euphoric.

"Oh, Jaine! I have good vibes about all this. Something tells me we're going to meet the men of our dreams!"

As you've no doubt already figured out, Lance's imagination tends to run on overdrive—especially when it comes to romance.

"Wouldn't it be great," he was saying, Disney stars practically twinkling in his eyes, "if we both wound up falling madly in love and had a double wedding?"

"Lance," I gently reminded him, "we haven't even met the guys yet. Don't you think you're getting a little ahead of yourself planning our weddings?"

"You're right, sweetie. Of course. First we've got to plan our bachelor and bachelorette parties! I'm thinking Vegas!"

I didn't even try to talk sense into him. Instead I did the only thing possible under the circumstances:

Finish his fries.

Chapter 6

Feeling guilty about all those chili cheese dog calories nestling on my thighs, I took a twenty-block walk when I got home that night. Okay, so it was ten blocks. Okay, six, if you must know. Which is about five and a half more than I'd walk if left to my own devices.

By the time I got back to my apartment, I was ready to eat the wallpaper.

And I wasn't the only one feeling peckish.

The minute I walked in the door, Prozac started weaving in and out around my ankles in her patented Feed Me dance.

Do you realize it's been a whole two and a half hours since my last snack? If I don't eat soon, I may faint.

"Oh, don't be such a drama queen," I said, trying to make my way to the kitchen without tripping over her.

I was just sloshing some Hearty Halibut Guts into her bowl, debating whether to order Chinese or pizza for my own dinner, when Joy called.

It turns out I was about to meet the man of my dreams a lot sooner than I thought.

"Fabulous news, Jaine!" Joy's voice came braying across the line. "I've just worked another dating miracle and fixed you up with one of L.A.'s most eligible bachelors!"

Ten to one, it was Barry the pocket protector guy.

"He's six feet tall, with blond hair, blue eyes, and homes in Malibu, Maui, and Palm Beach."

That sure didn't sound like Barry. Was it possible that for once in her life Joy had actually come through with a decent date?

"His name is Skip Holmeier III, and he's picking you up in half an hour."

A measly half hour? Well, that ruled out any last-minute liposuction.

"Now remember," Joy was saying. "My reputation is on the line here. You need to make a good impression. So whatever you do, don't wear elastic waist pants."

Oh, hell. She must have been talking to Lance.

After assuring her I would not leave the house with elastic clinging to my waist, I dashed into the shower to prep myself for my date with one of L.A.'s most eligible bachelors. I have to confess I was more than a tad excited. I stood under the shower spray, my cute new coif stuffed into a shower cap, trying to remember the few attractive male clients I'd seen on Joy's database and whether any of them had houses in Maui and Palm Beach. But my mind was a blank. Oh, well. I'd find out who he was soon enough.

Finished with my shower, I slipped on my undies and hurried to my closet, where I reached for a pair of non-elastic waist charcoal gray skinny pants I'd picked up half price at Nordstrom. Somehow I managed to close the button on its set-in waist, and put on a red merino wool tunic, some sterling silver dangly earrings, and my one and only pair of Manolo Blahniks.

Unfortunately I was unable to replicate Cassie's fabulous makeup job, so I just scrunched my curls, slapped on some lipstick and a bit of mascara, and hoped for the best.

"What do you think?" I asked, modeling my outfit for Prozac, who was stretched out on the living room sofa, giving herself one of her hourly gynecological exams.

She yawned a cavernous yawn.

I think it's time for a belly rub.

But there was no time for belly rubs. Because just then there was a knock on the door.

Omigosh. It was him! My Most Eligible Bachelor!

I took a deep breath and walked to the door.

And that's when I made my first mistake: I opened it.

Standing there was Skip Holmeier III.

How foolish I'd been to think Joy would actually come through for me.

True, he was six feet tall. And true, he had blond hair and blue eyes.

But I'm guessing he'd had those baby blues of his for at least seventy-five years. And that blond hair sitting on top of his head like a yellow bird's nest was most definitely a toupee.

For a crazy instant I allowed myself to hope that he was Skip's elderly chauffeur.

But, alas, that was not to be.

"Jaine!" he cried, his blue eyes twinkling through his cataracts. "I'm Skip Holmeier. What a pleasure to meet you!"

"Likewise, I'm sure," I gulped.

"For you, my dear," he said, handing me a nosebleed expensive bouquet of long-stemmed roses.

"Thanks so much," I managed to stammer. "Come on in, while I put these in water."

He stepped inside, and as he did, he suddenly clutched his chest.

Omigod. What if he was having a heart attack right here in my living room? If only I knew CPR. Or the

Heimlich maneuver. Or the name of a good cardiologist! I stood there, on the brink of calling 911, when I realized Skip wasn't having a heart attack.

He was merely staring, awestruck, at Prozac, who had gone back to examining her privates.

"Egad, what a beauty!"

Prozac looked up and preened.

So I've been told.

"She's the spitting image of Miss Marple!"

"Miss Marple?"

"My dearly departed cat," he explained and then raced to the sofa to scoop up Prozac in his liver-spotted arms.

"What's the little angel's name?" he asked.

"Prozac, and she's no little angel."

"Of course, she is. Aren't you, snookums?" he said to Prozac, rubbing his nose against hers.

She wriggled back in disgust.

Hey, buddy. Ever hear of breath mints?

Leaving Skip cooing sweet nothings in Prozac's ear, I went to the kitchen to put the roses in a vase.

I debated making a break for it from my kitchen window but eventually nixed the plan. Mainly because I don't have a kitchen window.

When I got back to the living room, Skip was still cooing.

"Why, you're the cutest snookums in Snookums Land. Yes, you are!"

"I'm the only one who's allowed to talk nauseating baby talk to my cat!" I felt like saying. But instead I just smiled brightly and said, "So! Where are we headed off to?"

He looked up at me vaguely, still in a love trance. And then he remembered.

"Oh, right. Our date. I made dinner reservations at Simon's."

Now it was my turn to go weak in the knees.

Simon's just happens to be one of the most expensive steak joints in L.A. And I, for one, could not wait to wrap myself around one of their juicy top sirloins.

But then I felt a twinge of guilt. Was it fair to make Skip pay for an expensive steak dinner when I knew I'd never go out with him again? Maybe I should just tell him I had a headache and cut the date short then and there.

Oh, what the heck? If his Rolex and fine Italian loafers were any indication, Skip was rolling in dough. Taking me for an expensive steak dinner would be the tiniest drop in his bucket of millions.

"Sounds wonderful!" I smiled.

Somehow Skip managed to tear himself away from Prozac.

"Parting is such sweet sorrow," he said, blowing her a kiss.

Prozac gazed up at him lazily.

Yeah, right. Whatever. Don't forget to bring back leftovers.

Tucking my arm into his elbow, Skip escorted me out to his car, a hulking monster of a Bentley, built no doubt when Queen Elizabeth was in diapers.

After a bit of a struggle, he managed to pull open the Brinks-like passenger door, and I slid onto an enormous bench seat, looking around for a seat belt.

"Afraid this model didn't come with seat belts," Skip explained.

Of course it didn't. They hadn't been invented then.

He popped around to the driver's side and spent several minutes squinting in the dim light, trying to fit his key in the ignition. Finally, I guided it into the right slot, and off we went.

Simon's was in the heart of Beverly Hills, about a five-minute drive from my duplex.

Five minutes, that is, when a normal person is driving the car.

Skip, however, maneuvered the *QE2* at a maddening fifteen miles an hour, humming to himself and ignoring the furious honks of the drivers behind us.

At long last we got to the restaurant. We could've walked faster.

I perked up, however, when Skip handed over the Bentley to the valet and we headed inside the posh steakerie. Instantly I was overcome by the heady aroma of prime steaks sizzling on a grill.

Dimly lit and very men's clubby, the place oozed old leather and new money.

Off in the bar, a jazz pianist was tinkling the ivories, while a tuxedo-clad maître d' stood vigil at a podium.

"Ah, good evening, Mr. Holmeier!" said the maître d', rushing to our side. "Right this way, sir."

Clearly Skip was one of his more valued patrons.

Visions of top sirloins danced in my head as the maître d' led us across the dining room. All around me I saw people digging into juicy T-bones. It was all I could do not to reach over and grab a bite.

The maître d' gestured to a prime corner booth, and I scooted into it, wondering if I should order bacon bits with my baked potato.

Skip slid in from the other side. For a minute I was afraid he was going to sidle up to me and make thigh contact, but much to my relief, he kept a respectable distance between us.

Even in the flattering glow of the restaurant's lighting,

I could see that his blond nest of a toupee did not match the graying shrub of real hair growing beneath it.

"So," Skip said when the maître d' had left us with our menus and slithered off to greet more carnivores. "Tell me all about yourself."

He flashed me what I was certain were a very expensive set of dentures.

"Well   " I began.

But before I could get out one syllable about Yours Truly, Skip butted in with: "And what about Prozac? How old is the little darling? How long have you had her? What do you feed her? Certainly not commercial cat food, I hope!"

His inquisition was cut short just then when our waiter came to take our order.

I was still debating about whether or not to order bacon bits with my baked potato when I heard Skip saying, "I'll have my usual, Maurice."

"The steamed vegetable plate, Mr. Holmeier?"

"Yes, indeed."

Was he kidding? What sort of nut ordered a steamed veggie plate in a steak restaurant?

"And for the lady?" our genial waiter inquired.

To my horror, Skip replied, "She'll have the same."

"What??" I gasped.

"Didn't Joy tell you?" he said, seeing the look of shock in my eyes. "I'm a strict vegan."

"No, she didn't happen to mention it."

"Well, I am, and I can't possibly allow you to pollute your body with red meat."

I sat on my hands to keep them from strangling him.

"Is it okay if I pollute my body with a glass of chardonnay?"

"Of course!" he chuckled. "Be sure it's organic," he

instructed Maurice. "Don't worry, Jaine," he said, turning back to me. "Simon's has the best steamed veggies in all of Los Angeles!"

Oh, well, I thought, staring enviously at a guy shoving a piece of steak into his mouth. At least I wouldn't have to worry about popping a button on my set-in waistband.

A busboy now appeared at our table with a basket of hot sourdough rolls and butter.

"No butter for us!" Skip instructed the busboy, waving away the butter crock.

I quickly grabbed a roll from the basket before he had that whisked away, too. I was just about to chomp down into it when I heard a familiar, "Yoo hoo!"

I looked up to see Joy tottering toward us on designer stilettos, cocooned in one of her billowing A-line dresses, honker sapphire earrings dangling from beneath an Early Streisand bob. Trotting alongside her like an obedient pup was Tonio, in black leather pants and a clinging white silk shirt. I wondered if the shirt was the two-hundred-dollar number he'd lusted after at Barneys.

"Hello, you two!" Joy cried in her Queen Mum voice. "Having fun?"

"Tons," I replied, squashing the urge to stab her with my unused butter knife.

"Jaine's such a delightful young woman," Skip enthused. "Do you know she has a cat who's the spitting image of Miss Marple?"

"Is that so?" Joy cooed.

Clearly eager to suck up to her wealthy client, Joy began blabbing about what a precious cat Miss Marple had been, telling a saccharine story about the time she played with Miss Marple while Skip was having his picture taken, feeding her ahi tuna and truffles and even some of the beluga caviar she kept hidden in her private refrigerator. She rambled on for a good sourdough roll and a half, extolling Miss Marple's many virtues.

"I swear, she was the most adorable cat I've ever seen!" she said, finally wrapping up her paean.

"She was, wasn't she?" Skip said, a far-off look in his eyes.

But Joy had forgotten all about Miss Marple.

"Look, Tonio!" she squealed with delight. "There's Greg Stanton!"

She pointed to a hunkalicious dude sitting at a nearby table. Slim and tan, with craggy cheekbones and a headful of thick, sun-bleached hair, he looked like the guy voted "Most Handsome" in a Tommy Hilfiger photo shoot. Practically glued to his side was a stunning brunet, feeding him the olive from her martini.

Joy turned to me and breathily informed me, "Greg's one of the most successful artists on the West Coast. Does fabulously colorful landscapes."

"A very talented fellow," Skip agreed.

"And he's one of my most loyal clients," Joy said with pride.

Huh? I had to wonder why on earth a gorgeous guy like Greg Stanton would need Joy's services.

"Yoo hoo, Greg!" she called out, her sapphire earrings jangling as she waved.

Greg tore his eyes away from his brunet and, noticing Joy, offered up a feeble smile. Like most people who came in contact with Joy, he didn't exactly seem thrilled to see her.

But if Joy sensed his lack of enthusiasm, she showed no sign of it.

"We positively must go say hello. Mustn't we, Tonio?"

"Okay," Tonio muttered. "But let's not stand around gabbing forever. I wanna eat."

You're not the only one, I felt like telling him.

"Be good, you two," Joy said to me and Skip with a most disgusting wink, and then trotted off to hound Greg Stanton.

I spent the rest of the dinner in culinary hell, watching a parade of steaks sail past me, stuck with a plate of crummy steamed veggies.

The meal slogged on for what seemed like an eternity but was in reality only fifty-seven minutes and thirty-two seconds. (I was counting.) During which time Skip treated me to a recitation of The Life and Times of Skip Holmeier—starting with his kindergarten years, his stint at Stanford, his four decades at the brokerage firm of Holmeier & Holmeier, his endless charitable works, and his stultifyingly boring stamp collection. And, of course, his slavish devotion to the late Miss Marple, the patter of whose little paws had been like music to Skip's ears.

Because he talked so much, it took him forever to finish his damn veggies. At one point, I was *thisclose* to stabbing my fork into his cauliflower and shoving it down his throat.

Eventually he finished his veggie plate, and I practically wept with relief when he signaled Maurice for the check.

At last my long ordeal was over.

Or so I thought.

We were on our way out of the restaurant when Skip looked over at the bar area, where the jazz pianist was still tinkling the ivories.

Stopping dead in his tracks, Skip clutched his heart. Once again, I was bracing myself for a coronary.

But, no. Skip was fine.

"The piano player," he said. "He's playing 'Misty.' "

And so he was, a very lovely rendition of it.

"That was Miss Marple's favorite song," Skip said, blinking back tears.

(In case you're interested, Miss Marple's favorite movie was *Three Coins in the Fountain*, and her favorite TV show was *Green Acres*. All fun facts I'd gleaned during dinner.)

"Let's go listen," Skip pleaded.

I was about to say no, but then I saw something that made me change my mind—large bowls of mixed nuts on the tables.

After the anemic plate of steamed veggies I'd choked down for dinner, those nuts looked mighty tempting.

"Okay," I said. "But just for a few minutes."

Skip led me to a table right up front near the pianist, who was still belting out "Misty."

The minute we sat down, I reached for the bowl of nuts and held on to them with a viselike grip.

Take these away, I felt like warning Skip, *and you're a dead man.*

But Skip wasn't interested in the nuts. His eyes were closed, lost no doubt in memories of Miss Marple.

We gave our orders to a cocktail waitress: celery tonic for Skip and organic chardonnay for moi.

The minute she was gone, I wasted no time diving into those nuts, picking out the cashews first, then chomping down on some Brazil nuts. I offered some to Skip, but thank heavens, he waved them away.

I'd just finished fishing out a particularly tasty Brazil nut when I looked up and saw the piano player staring at me and smiling in a most seductive manner.

Good heavens. Was he actually flirting with me?

Skip seemed to think so.

"I don't like the way that man is looking at you," he

said, glaring at the piano player and taking a stiff shot of his celery tonic.

"Don't be silly," I whispered. "I'm sure he smiles at all the patrons."

But I was wrong. The handsome, dark-haired pianist kept his eyes on me, and me only, all the while beaming me his seductive smile.

Hmm. Maybe this date wasn't turning out so bad, after all. Maybe the pianist would turn out to be the man of my dreams, and maybe someday we'd be telling our grandchildren how we fell in love at first sight over a bowl of mixed nuts.

"No, I don't like it," Skip was saying, shooting daggers at the piano player. "Not one bit. He's got a nerve staring at you like that."

"I'm sure it means nothing, Skip," I said, praying I was wrong.

We sat through a few more tunes, Skip growing angrier with each slug of his celery tonic. Finally when the pianist had not taken his eyes off me for twelve consecutive minutes, Skip banged down his glass.

"That does it!" he cried, getting up.

"Please, Skip. People are staring."

And indeed everyone in the joint was looking at him.

But Skip didn't care.

Shoving back his chair, he stomped over to the piano player.

"My good man," he sputtered, "I resent the way you have been leering at my fiancée all night."

His *fiancée*???

I almost choked on a filbert.

Since when had we gotten engaged? Was it possible he'd proposed during dinner and I'd missed it? Had I dozed off some time during the cauliflower course?

"I may be of advanced years," Skip was saying, "but

I am a master in the art of fisticuffs. Shall we take this out into the alley?"

"Okay, dude," said the handsome pianist, smiling serenely, "but first I'm going to have to get Lucy."

Lucy? We hadn't even gone on our first date, and already there was another woman.

"C'mere, Lucy, honey!"

And then out from behind a curtain came a dog with a harness. The pianist got up and reached for a cane I'd failed to notice on top of his piano.

Yikes. Lucy was a Seeing Eye dog, and the guy who'd fallen in love with me at first sight was blind.

Cancel that honeymoon.

"I'm so sorry, my good man," Skip said, tossing a fifty-dollar bill in the tip jar. "I had no idea. . . ."

He rejoined me at our table and all around us, I could hear people buzzing in pity for the poor piano player, outraged at the scene Skip had just caused.

"I don't care how old he is. He's still a bully," I heard one lady say.

"And what about his date?" I heard her husband reply. "Did you see the way she sucked up those nuts? Like a vacuum cleaner."

I sat there, shrinking with embarrassment as my former true love finished his set.

"Shall we go?" Skip asked brightly when it was all over, as if he hadn't just humiliated himself (and moi) in front of a roomful of jazz lovers.

Head bowed in shame, I followed Skip out the door, ignoring the dirty looks boring into our backs.

"Care for a nut?" I heard someone snicker behind my back.

"Nah," another wise guy cried out. "She's already dating one."

A perfect ending to my Date of Joy.

*   *   *

Joy sprang from her office to greet me when I showed up at work the next day, eager to hear about my date with Skip.

"So how was it?" she asked.

"Like the *Hindenburg*, with cauliflower."

Okay, so what I really said was:

"Skip's a very nice guy, but I don't think I want to see him again."

"Oh, but you have to! It's a Dates of Joy rule. You've got to give every potential love mate at least three chances."

Oh, no. No way in hell was I going out with Skip again. A girl has her limits.

"Sorry, Joy. I'm a writer, not a member of your club. You set me up so I could get a picture of how the club works. I got the picture. I don't need to see any more."

I stood back and braced myself for Hurricane Joy to strike again.

But much to my surprise, she pursed her lips in a pout and put on a Poor Me look.

"Oh, dear," she sighed. "Skip's a very important client. I need to stay on his good side. And he really likes you. He already called to tell me so. If I throw in an extra five hundred bucks to your pay, will you follow my three-date rule?"

Good Lord. Did she actually think I was the kind of woman who'd pimp myself out and date a man I had absolutely no interest in for a few extra dollars?

If so, she knew me well.

"Three dates, it is," I said with a feeble smile.

Oh, don't go shaking your head like that.

Somebody had to pay to keep Prozac up to her furry little neck in Hearty Halibut Guts. And I don't see you opening your wallet, do I?

YOU'VE GOT MAIL!

To: Jausten
From: DaddyO
Subject: Magnificent Gift!

Wonderful news, Lambchop! I've just bought your mom
the most magnificent Valentine's Day gift. A genuine pink
diamond ring! For only fifty bucks! What a bargain, huh? I
got it from a guy in the parking lot at Costco who gets
his stuff wholesale and passes on the savings to his
customers. I can't wait to see your mom's face when she
opens the box!

Love 'n' snuggles from,
Daddy

To: Jausten
From: Shoptillyoudrop
Subject: All I Really Want

Daddy's been dropping hints all week about what a
fabulous Valentine's gift he bought me. Frankly,
sweetheart, all I really want for Valentine's Day is a
nice dinner at Le Chateaubriand where Daddy doesn't go
running off to the bar every five minutes to check the
sports scores.

XOXO,
Mom

To: Jausten
From: DaddyO
Subject: A New Leaf

I've been giving it some thought, Lambchop, and I may have overreacted just a tad the other day at the clubhouse. Mom insists that all Lester was doing was giving her a palm reading, and I'm inclined to believe her. After all, your mother is a woman of sterling moral values. And Lester may be an insufferable gasbag, but he couldn't possibly have the gall to make a pass at Mom, especially in a community like Tampa Vistas, where gossip travels at the speed of light. I guess I was rather foolish to overreact. Must make a note to turn over a new leaf and rein in my emotions in the future.

Oops. Gotta run. Your mom's calling me.

Love 'n' hugs from,
Daddy

To: Jausten
From: DaddyO
Subject: The Gasbag Romeo Strikes Again!

You won't believe what your mom just found on our doorstep: Two dozen pink roses. The card said, "Happy Valentine's Day from Your Secret Admirer."

Well, we all know who that is. The gasbag Romeo has struck again! If he thinks I'm going to sit by quietly as he flirts with your mother, he's got another think coming!

Your outraged,
Daddy

To: Jausten
From: Shoptillyoudrop
Subject: My Secret Admirer

Omigosh, honey. Somebody just left two dozen of the most glorious pink roses on our doorstep. The card was signed, "From Your Secret Admirer." There was no florist's name on the card, so we have no way of finding out who sent them. Daddy's convinced they're from Lester Pinkus.

Oh, heavens. Could Daddy possibly be right?

Does Lester Pinkus have a secret crush on me?

Love and XXX
From your very rattled,
Mom

Chapter 7

I must admit I was a tad shocked to read my parents' e-mails the next morning. I'd thought for sure Lester Pinkus's "crush" on Mom was all a figment of Daddy's imagination. But now I had my doubts.

Did Lester actually send Mom those two dozen roses? Was he her Secret Admirer? Would Daddy make it through the day without challenging him to a duel?

Only time—and the next couple of chapters—will tell.

All thoughts of my parents' love triangle vanished into the ether, however, when I showed up at the office and found Joy in the middle of a major meltdown.

It seems her sapphire earrings, the ones I'd seen her wearing at Simon's the other night, had gone missing. And now Joy was stomping around the office, curses flying, ready to call in Scotland Yard to nab the thieves. If you asked me, she probably misplaced them. But Joy was only too happy to pin the blame on someone else. Anyone else. The plumbers who'd come to her condo to fix a leak. Her weekly maid service. Even poor Travis came under suspicion, having been unlucky enough to have delivered some dry cleaning to her condo the previous afternoon.

After much deliberation, she decided the culprits were the gals at Mighty Maids Maid Service.

"I'm going to sue those bastards for every cent they're worth!" she said, getting on the phone with her attorney.

I wisely spent the day trying to stay under her radarscope, working on fictitious dating profiles. At around five p.m. I made a break for it, whispering my good-byes to Cassie and Travis.

Out in the hallway I sprinted for the elevator and waited impatiently for it to come. It finally showed up, and I was just about to step inside when I heard Joy's familiar screech:

"Yoo hoo, Jaine! Hold that elevator!"

Oh, groan. For an instant I debated pretending I didn't hear her. But, coward that I was, I didn't have the nerve. So I held open the elevator doors as she came puffing to join me. I rode down with her, listening to her blather about the evil vixens at Mighty Maids, all the while inhaling the asphyxiating scent of her designer perfume.

When at last the doors opened and we made our way to the small parking lot out back, I gulped the fresh air gratefully.

"Those thieving maids will rot in hell when I'm through with them!" Joy was ranting when suddenly an older-model Mercedes came roaring into the lot and, with a squeal of brakes, lurched to a stop in front of us.

A tall, raven-haired gal emerged from the car, her animal-print dress pulled tight around her stick-thin frame. She tossed her great mane of ebony tresses— most of which I suspected were extensions—and planted herself in front of us.

Up close I could see her skin had been pulled tauter than a snare drum, her eyebrows immovable as Mount Rushmore. Clearly she'd put some lucky plastic surgeon's kids through college, and probably grad school.

"Why the hell haven't you returned my calls?" she asked Joy, her eyes flashing anger.

"Do I know you?" Joy replied in her snootiest Queen Mum voice.

"Yes, you know me. I'm one of your clients. Alyce Winters."

"The name sounds familiar," Joy conceded.

"It should. I've been leaving you messages every day for the past two weeks."

"I've been busy," Joy replied with a careless shrug.

"Six months ago I forked over ten grand for your so-called dating service. You promised you'd introduce me to my choice of millionaires, and so far I've had exactly one date—with a dumpy insurance salesman from Downey who spent half the date trying to sell me a term life policy."

If you expected Joy to be contrite, think again. Never an empathetic soul on the best of days, Joy was now in an especially foul Mighty Maids-induced mood.

With all the tact and sensitivity of a rabid pit bull, she snarled, "Hey, honey. In case you haven't noticed, you're not exactly a painting in the Louvre."

Alyce gasped.

"You're not fooling anyone with those hair extensions and that bargain-basement facelift. I'm a matchmaker, not a miracle worker. The insurance salesman was the best I could do for a Botoxed old bag like you."

I'm sure Alyce's face would have been contorted with rage if her muscles hadn't been frozen solid.

There was, however, no mistaking the fire burning in her eyes.

"How dare you?" she managed to sputter.

"This is how," said Joy.

With that, she gave her a powerful shove, which sent Alyce reeling up against a nearby Camry.

"Get lost, loser!" Joy screeched. "And don't bother me again. You're officially banned from Dates of Joy!"

Alyce and I watched in stunned disbelief as Joy marched over to her silver Jaguar, flung herself inside, and zoomed away.

"Never in my life has anyone ever talked to me like that." Alyce's lips somehow managed to bust through her filler and began trembling.

"I'm so sorry," I tsked. "Would you like an Almond Joy?" I started fishing around in my purse for a bar I'd been snacking on earlier that afternoon. "I'm afraid I may have already taken a bite or two, but you can eat it from the other end."

The offer of chocolate, usually a foolproof antidepressant, failed to cheer her up.

"No, thanks," she said woodenly, brushing herself off and heading for her Mercedes.

As she walked away, I couldn't help noticing she was crying.

The rest of her facial muscles may have been Botoxed to oblivion, but her tear ducts were working just fine.

I drove home, unable to forget those tears rolling down Alyce Winters's cheeks. How could Joy have treated her so cruelly? The more I thought about it, the angrier I got. By the time I got back to my apartment, I'd decided to quit my gig with Dates of Joy.

Yes, my mind was made up. And it stayed that way for a whole thirteen and a half seconds—until I saw the small mountain of unpaid bills piled up on my dining room table.

Oh, dear. As much as I wanted to, I simply could not afford to walk away from Joy Amoroso.

After sloshing some Minced Mackerel Guts into Prozac's dinner bowl, I made a beeline for the fridge to pour myself a much-needed glass of chardonnay. I had just taken a few sips (okay, gulps) when the phone rang.

Wearily, I trotted over to answer it.

I did not think it was possible for my spirits to sink any lower, but the voice at the other end of the line sent them plummeting.

"Hello, sweetheart." Oh, gaak. It was Skip Holmeier. "How's my favorite green eyed gal?"

"My eyes are hazel."

"Actually I was talking about Prozac."

"Oh. She's fine."

"So glad to hear it! She's such an adorable kitty! Give her my love—and kisses, too."

"Will do," I said, rolling my eyes.

"Anyhow, I'm calling because"—here he paused for a phlegm-filled clearing of his throat—"I was wondering if you wanted to see me again."

Only from a Hubble telescope.

"I was thinking next Thursday? For lunch?"

Ordinarily under these circumstances I'd make up a tiny fib and tell him I was moving to Tasmania or had just fallen in love with the woman of my dreams. But if you recall, I'd sold my soul to Joy for an extra five hundred bucks and had agreed to her Three Date rule.

"Um, sure," I said, with a marked lack of enthusiasm.

"Wonderful! I'll pick you up around one."

Oh, well, I told myself as I hung up. I had to think positive thoughts. Maybe the date would be fun. Maybe I'd gain new insights on the elderly. Maybe I'd be able to sneak in a butter pat on my steamed veggies.

I was headed for the kitchen to pour myself a wee bit more chardonnay when I heard Lance banging at my front door.

Like a fool, I opened it.

"It's official!" Lance cried, sailing in on Cloud Nine.

"I'm in love! My date with Donny Johnson was absolutely divine!" He grabbed my wine and took a healthy slug. "You'll never guess what we did!"

"If it involves handcuffs and whipped cream, I don't want to hear about it."

He shot me a wounded look.

"Jaine, please. Our date was perfectly innocent. Donny and I went for a long walk on the beach, then stopped off for dinner at an intimate little Italian restaurant, where they played old Dean Martin records and Donny wrote *I Love You* on the tablecloth with his ziti. Isn't that the most romantic thing you ever heard?"

"Yes, nothing says love like pasta on a tablecloth."

"And look what Donny gave me!" he said, ignoring my snippet of sarcasm.

He held out his wrist, revealing a magnificent stainless steel watch dotted with what looked like diamonds. "A genuine Rolex. It had to cost at least five grand!"

"Wow, it's gorgeous!"

Lance grinned in triumph. "And you said he wasn't a real millionaire!"

Was it possible? Was Lance the first person in Dates of Joy history to have actually gone on a date of joy?

"And what about you?" Lance asked. "How did your date go?"

"An utter disaster," I sighed. "The guy was not only old enough to be Methuselah's grandfather, he drove his Bentley two miles an hour, made me eat a veggie plate at a steak restaurant, and picked a fight with a blind piano player."

"He drives a Bentley? How divine!"

"Have you not listened to a word I've just said? The guy's an old fart vegan nutcase!"

"With a *Bentley!* Really, Jaine. Some day you must learn to get your priorities straight!"

I grabbed my wine back and finished it in one exasperated gulp.

"Would you look at the time?" Lance cried, flashing his Rolex in my face. "Must dash to get dressed for my date with Donny. He's taking me to the ballet. You know how I adore the ballet."

"Drooling over men in tights does not make you a ballet lover, Lance."

"Oh, my. Somebody woke up on the bitchy side of the bed this morning. But don't worry, sweetie," he said as he headed for the door. "I forgive you. You're just jealous because I found true love, and you got stuck with a loony old fart."

I stuck out my tongue at his retreating back.

I hate it when he's right.

Chapter 8

The next few days passed in an aggravating blur as Joy got ready for her annual Valentine's Singles Mixer.

Or as she so modestly put it, "*The* singles party of the year!"

In full-tilt tyrant mode, Joy proceeded to drive Cassie and Travis crazy, barking orders at them as they transformed the Dates of Joy photo studio into a party venue.

After cramming all the photo equipment into the small kitchen adjacent to the studio, Travis and Cassie got up on ladders to string crepe paper across the room. A job that would normally take about a half hour took forever as Joy shrieked conflicting directions at them.

"Higher! No, lower! Now just a bit to the right! No, no! To the left! No, to the right again!"

Through it all, I sat at a computer in the reception area, banging out phony dating profiles.

When the crepe paper was finally hung, Cassie spent hours on the phone, trying to line up discount balloons and making arrangements with the caterer, a guy Joy dug up on Craigslist.

"He told Joy he was the former executive chef at

Coachella Prison," Cassie whispered to me. "Frankly, I suspect he was an inmate."

Meanwhile, Travis was hard at work at his computer, making counterfeit copies of Dom Pérignon champagne labels.

"Joy buys the cheapest champagne she can find," he explained, "and then has me paste on phony labels."

I shook my head in disbelief.

The woman never ceased to amaze me.

Finally Friday rolled around, the day before Joy's Valentine's Day Singles Mixer.

I'd just wrapped up my final fictitious dating profile for a male model I'd dubbed Anton Zeller (a Santa Barbara native who, when not running his highly successful chain of teeth whitening salons, loved surfing, motorbiking, and Charlotte Brontë novels).

I could not wait to go home and spend the next few hours—if not the entire weekend—soaking in a hot tub, washing away the stress of these past few days.

I was just packing up my things when Joy swooped down on me, noshing on a chocolate from her Godiva box.

"By the way, Jaine, I expect you to be at the mixer tomorrow night."

Oh, no. No way. This was *not* going to happen.

"Honestly, Joy. I've got more than enough material for the brochure. I don't think I need to be at the party."

"Well, I think you do. So be there. And if anyone asks, you're a satisfied client."

Her one and only.

"And speaking of the brochure," Joy added, a nasty glint in her eye, "I expect your copy on my desk tomorrow morning."

"You need the brochure copy tomorrow? Saturday?"

"Yes. You have a problem with that?"

"I haven't had time to even start the brochure. I've been too busy writing your blankety-blank bios."

This is a family novel, so I am sparing you the actual blankety-blank words involved. But I can assure you, they were pretty ripe.

"Well, better get cracking." She popped another Godiva in her mouth. "I need it on my desk tomorrow."

Grrr. I came *thisclose* to ramming her with Travis's stapler. But I didn't want to waste the staples.

Knowing Joy, she'd charge me for them.

"That godawful woman!" I cried, stomping into my apartment. "Taking up weeks of my life with her stupid dating profiles, and then just when I thought I could sit back and relax for five minutes, she gives me less than a day to write a sixteen-page brochure!"

Prozac leaped down from the sofa where she'd been snoring and hurried to my side.

Yeah, right. Whatever. Do I smell shrimp with lobster sauce?

Indeed she did. I'd stopped off for Chinese take-out on my way home. And now Prozac was practically bonding herself to my ankles, yowling to be fed.

I gave up any hope of getting her to eat the Savory Salmon Entrails I'd been planning to feed her, and instead sloshed some shrimp into her bowl.

Gone in sixty seconds.

It didn't take me too much longer to polish off my chow.

Around about now, if there were any justice in this world, I'd be sinking down into a strawberry-scented bubble bath, listening to the mellow sounds of Diana Krall and throwing mental darts at Joy Amoroso.

But life is not just. (As anyone who's ever been on a blind date with Skip Holmeier can well attest.)

I had no time for soaking in tubs. Not with a sixteen-page brochure to write.

Pouring myself an eensy glass of wine—okay, so it wasn't so eensy—I sat down at my computer and stared at the blank screen.

Oh, what I'd give to write the truth about Joy, about what a double-dealing, low-life excuse for a human being she was.

And before I knew it, that's exactly what I was doing.

I don't know what came over me. Maybe it was my long simmering anger, my sense of outraged injustice. Probably it was just the chardonnay.

But suddenly I was writing the truth.

And it went something like this:

> *Are you looking for the love of your life? A warm, supportive mentor to guide you through the minefields of dating? Then whatever you do, stay away from Joy Amoroso, the Psycho Cupid of Beverly Hills. The woman is to dating what Hitler was to Bar Mitzvahs. . . .*

My fingers flew over the keyboard as I spilled the beans about how Joy charged outrageous membership fees for services rarely rendered, how she padded her database with phony pictures of actors and models, how she browbeat her employees, and worst of all, how after nearly two weeks of working with her, she hadn't offered me a single chocolate!

I read my copy out loud to Prozac, who looked up

from where she was sprawled on the sofa and gave me an encouraging thump of her tail.

You go, girl!

Okay, all she really did was yawn, but it seemed like an enthusiastic yawn.

Then I had a great idea. I'd add pictures to my copy!

Ladies, I wrote, *here's the kind of guy you can expect to meet at Dates of Joy.*

With the help of my good buddies at Google Images, I was soon adorning my brochure with pictures of Norman Bates, Hannibal Lecter, and Elmer Fudd.

And guys, just check out these nifty gals in Joy's dating file.

Here I pasted pictures of The Bride of Frankenstein, Lizzie Borden, and Honey Boo Boo.

After several more damning paragraphs, I checked my watch and saw it was close to eleven p.m.

Oh, foo. Looked like the party was over.

It was great fun while it lasted, but now I had to write the real stuff.

So I knuckled down and spent the next several hours churning out the adulatory copy Joy was paying me to write, regurgitating all her pap about how matchmaking was in her blood and how it was her life mission to connect soul mates. I wrote about her fictitious track record of successful hookups. And about her equally fictitious gifts of empathy, sensitivity, and compassion. All of which combined to make her a matchmaker par excellence, a caring cupid with a heart of gold.

When I was finished, I practically needed a diabetes shot.

It was way over the top, but I knew Joy would eat it up. Worse, she'd probably believe it.

By now it was after two a.m. Beyond exhausted, I

didn't even bother to run a spell check. I just popped it off in an e-mail, thrilled to be rid of it.

And so it was with happy heart that I toddled off to bed, blissfully unaware of the poop that was waiting in the wings, about to hit my fan.

Chapter 9

Valentine's Day dawned bright and sunny, the birds chirping merrily outside my window.

(It was easy for them to be merry. They didn't have to haul their sorry fannies to Joy's party that night.)

What with all the hoo-ha of working for Joy, I'd been sadly neglecting my household chores, so I spent the entire day dusting, vacuuming, and catching up on my laundry.

And if you believe that, I've got some shares in Enron I'd like to sell you.

I'm not ashamed to confess I lolled around in my pj's the entire day, doing the *New York Times* crossword puzzle and leafing through the Fudge of the Month catalog.

It was heaven, sheer heaven.

But eventually, it was time to get dressed for Joy's Valentine's mixer.

Grudgingly I hauled myself to my closet and tossed on some slacks and a sweater. Gray, to match my mood. And in an act of defiance, I chose a pair of slacks with an elastic waist. Worn out elastic, at that.

So there, Joy Amoroso!

Other than a splash of lipstick, I didn't bother with

makeup, and corralled my mop of curls into a messy ponytail.

Tossing Prozac some Hearty Halibut Guts for her dinner, I carefully refrained from chowing down on some leftover pot stickers that were sitting in the refrigerator, calling my name. (Okay, so I ate one, but that's all. I swear. Okay, two, if you must know.)

I intended to stuff myself silly with hors d'oeuvres at the mixer, determined to make Joy pay in some small way for all the aggravation she'd put me through.

Checking my watch, I saw it was 7:45. The party started at eight, and I planned on getting there late. The less time I had to spend with Joy, the happier I'd be. So to kill time, I decided to read over the brochure copy I'd e-mailed Joy the night before.

I clicked on the file and cringed to read my gloppy words of praise. If anyone on the planet didn't deserve them, it was Joy. I was about to log off when suddenly I noticed a splotch of color down at the bottom of the page.

I scrolled down, and to my horror, I saw the puffy-cheeked face of Elmer Fudd!

Omigod! I'd been in such a rush last night, I never deleted the joke copy I'd originally written, the zinger-laden manifesto where I'd called Joy a "Psycho Cupid."

If Joy saw this, I could kiss my paycheck good-bye.

No doubt about it. My poop had landed. And I was knee deep in the stuff.

I drove over to the party like Dale Earnhardt on uppers, my heart racing almost as fast as my engine. I prayed that Joy hadn't yet read my e-mail and that Travis would know her password so that I could delete it.

The mixer was well under way when I showed up at

the Dates of Joy photo studio, now festooned with streamers and discount balloons. Desperate singles were wandering around with glazed looks in their eyes, wondering no doubt what happened to all the stunning people they'd seen in Joy's date book.

Cassie, her purple hair striped red for the occasion, was working the room as a waitress, serving hors d'oeuvres from a tray. Travis, in a white shirt and bow tie, stood behind a makeshift bar, pouring phony Dom Pérignon into champagne glasses.

I was just about to hurry to his side when Joy came bursting out from the kitchen, dressed head to toe in Valentine's red: Red tent dress, red designer shoes, even a red bow in her hair. Pinned to her ample bosom was a huge button that read I ME.

At last. Truth in advertising.

She took one look at me and came charging at me like a rhino in Jimmy Choos.

Damn. It was too late. She'd read my e-mail.

I braced myself for the volcano that was about to erupt.

"Where the hell have you been?" she hissed. "I've been looking all over for you. The idiotic caterer didn't bring any waitstaff, and I need you to help Cassie serve the hors d'oeuvres."

Thank heavens! I was safe! For the time being, anyway.

"Of course, Joy. Anything you say."

She sent me to the kitchen, where her caterer, a burly guy named Carl, handed me an apron emblazoned with the logo FRUGAL FIXIN'S. Carl took great pride in informing me that he was the former executive chef at Coachella Prison. Although, as Cassie had said, he did indeed look like he could have been one of the inmates.

"Here you go," he said, handing me a tray of delicious stuffed mushrooms. I happened to know they were delicious, because I popped one in my mouth as I headed back to the party.

I hadn't taken two steps into the room when suddenly Joy materialized at my side.

"No eating on the job!" she snapped.

So much for my plan to snack my way through her party.

But who cared? Just as long as I was able to delete that dratted e-mail.

I wandered around with my tray, waiting for my opportunity to approach Travis and ask him for Joy's password. But Joy was eyeing me like a hawk. If she saw me standing around talking to Travis, she'd be on me like hot fudge on a potato chip.

(You've never tried it? It's delicious.)

Not even the arrival of Tonio was enough to distract Joy. Clad in his usual tight leather pants and chest-baring shirt, Tonio sidled over to give Joy a peck on her cheek. Much to my surprise, I saw her body stiffen. Through gritted teeth, she said something to him—something that made his face turn ashen. Then she turned and stalked off in a huff.

Uh-oh. I smelled trouble in paradise.

By now the room was crowded with lonely singles, still looking in vain for the gorgeous soul mates Joy had promised them.

"Where are all the handsome men I saw on her Web site?" I heard one mousy brunet moan to another.

"Omigosh," her friend replied. "Here's one of them now!"

I followed her gaze.

Standing in the doorway was Greg Stanton, the hunkalicious artist I'd seen at Simon's Steak House. Slim and tan in jeans and a turtleneck, his sun-bleached hair bringing out the deep blue of his eyes, he was a stunner of the highest order.

Once again I wondered why a guy like Greg needed Joy's services.

Joy was instantly at his side, linking her elbow in his in a viselike grip.

"Greg, my deah!" she squealed in Queen Mum mode. "How veddy lovely to see you!"

Gazing up at him and batting her eyelashes coquettishly, she was—at last—distracted.

Taking advantage of the moment, I dashed over to the bar where Travis was busy trying to keep the phony Dom Pérignon labels from slipping off their bottles as they sloshed around in the ice bucket.

"Hey, Jaine!" he said, catching sight of me. "What can I get you?"

"Joy's password."

"Huh?"

"It's a long, awful story, Travis, but I wrote some horrible things about Joy and sent them to her by mistake. Now I need to get into her e-mail. I'm just praying you know her password."

"Yeah, sure. Of course. It's CuteCupid."

"Oh, gaak."

"My sentiments, exactly."

Filled with gratitude, I slipped Travis a Frugal Fixin's mushroom cap.

Now all I had to do was dash across the reception area to Joy's inner office.

But how? Joy had relinquished her grip on Greg, who was now surrounded by a gaggle of admirers. Which meant Joy was back on patrol duty, eyes in the back of her head on high alert. I couldn't risk having her see me put down my tray and leave the room.

I continued to perform waitress duty for the next half

hour or so. Every time I looked over at Joy, I saw her glaring at me.

Good Lord, did she have nothing better to do than make sure I didn't eat one of her precious hors d'oeuvres?

I was beginning to think I'd never escape her eagle eyes when at last I got a break.

Having run out of hors d'oeuvres, I went to the kitchen to get a refill. But Carl was running behind, and the latest batch of goodies—spinach and cheese-filled filo dough—was still baking.

When Joy saw me coming out from the kitchen with an empty tray, she went ballistic.

"What the hell is wrong with that guy?" she exploded. "That's the last time I ever hire an ex-con to cater a party."

So Cassie was right. Carl *was* an ex-con!

As Joy took off to the kitchen to give him hell, I threw my empty tray down on the bar and charged out past the reception area into Joy's office.

I practically wept with relief at the sight of her laptop on her desk.

Plopping my fanny in her antique desk chair, I typed her password into her e-mail account.

Bingo! I was in.

With trembling fingers, I clicked onto her e-mails. There it was. My Dates of Joy brochure.

I opened the e-mail and scrolled down to see E. Fudd, H. Lecter, and the rest of the gang smiling up at me.

"Sorry, guys," I muttered. "You're history."

And then, with the greatest of pleasure, I zapped my slanderous brochure to oblivion.

Mission accomplished.

True, I would have to face the wrath of Joy for not getting the brochure in on time, but that was a small price to pay. In fact, if I hurried home from the party and re-sent the e-mail later that night, she'd probably never even know the difference.

I sat back, limp with relief, when I noticed Joy's prized Godivas on her desk. I was just about to do the unthinkable and reach for one when I heard footsteps thundering toward Joy's office.

Oh, crud. They sounded an awful lot like Jimmy Choos on a rampage.

"Shut up, Tonio!" cried an unmistakable voice.

It was Joy, all right.

I looked around for a place to hide and saw absolutely nothing.

So I hurled myself under Joy's desk. Thank heavens it had a blocked front.

Curled up with my knees rammed into my chest, I looked around and saw that I was surrounded by dust bunnies the size of Chihuahuas—not to mention a moldy pair of slippers and an old M&M's wrapper.

There I was, cowering amid the dust bunnies, breathing in the heady aroma of Joy's foot funk, when the door banged open.

"Joy, honey!" Tonio was wailing. "I can explain everything."

"Forget it, Tonio," I heard Joy snarl in reply. "I know what you did, and I'm turning you in to the authorities."

"But, sugarplum!"

"Don't sugarplum me, you low-life greaseball!"

As I listened avidly to this heated exchange, wondering what on earth Tonio had done to stir up Joy's wrath, I suddenly felt my nose begin to itch. Oh, hell. I was going to sneeze!

Damn those dust bunnies!

Quickly I pressed my finger under my nose, trying desperately to stem the explosion that was building up inside.

"Can't we please just talk this over?" Tonio pleaded.

"Too late. We're through. Finito. You'll never go shopping at Barneys again!"

"But, Joy—"

"I can't waste any more time talking about this. I've got to get back to the party."

Yes! Go! Go back to the party!

I waited for the sounds of her designer-clad feet stomping out the door, but I waited in vain.

"No, wait," she was saying. "I need an aspirin."

An aspirin? Couldn't she just suffer like everyone around her?

"Dealing with all those pathetic losers out there has given me a splitting headache."

Then before I knew it, she was sitting at her desk, her Jimmy Choos just inches from my torturously itchy nose.

Please, Lord. Don't let her look down and see me!

I sat there, crunched in a ball and staring at Joy's toe cleavage as she rummaged around, slamming desk drawers, looking for her dratted aspirin.

By now the itch in my nose was unbearable.

Any minute now I'd be sneezing on her Jimmy Choos!

"Oh, here it is!" she finally said, music to my ears.

Rattling her aspirin bottle, she got up and headed for the door, but not before grabbing a Godiva for the road.

"Thank God for chocolate," I heard her mutter, her mouth full of candy. "That's one thing I can always count on."

"But, honey bun," Tonio cooed, "you know you can always count on me, too."

"Don't make me laugh." Joy snorted.

And off she stomped, Tonio at her heels, begging for another chance to talk things over.

Finally, I was alone. Just me, the dust bunnies, and Joy's stinky slippers.

I took my finger out from under my nose, prepared to let loose with a Vesuvius-sized explosion.

But wouldn't you know?

Now that Joy was gone, I didn't have to sneeze anymore.

After waiting a few minutes to make sure Joy and Tonio were not returning for an encore performance, I unfurled myself from my fetal position and crawled out from under the desk.

So eager was I to get the heck out of there that I foolishly raced into the reception area without checking to see if the coast was clear—only to bump smack dab into Greg Stanton.

Oh, foo. I couldn't risk having him tell Joy I'd been skulking around in her office.

"Hi, there!" I chirped, trying my best to look wide-eyed and innocent. "I suppose you're wondering what I was doing in Joy's office."

"Not really."

"Just in case you were, I was looking for my purse. I thought I might have left it there. So that's what I was doing. Just looking for my purse is all. You know how it is, you put your purse down one minute and the next you can't remember where the heck it is. Then again, I guess you wouldn't know. It's a lady thing."

I tend to babble when I'm nervous.

"Well, I hope you find it."

"Find what?"

"Your purse."

"Oh, right. My purse."

He shot me a most skeptical look, and I could feel his gorgeous blue eyes boring into my back as I trotted off to the party.

In spite of my encounter with Greg, I returned to the mixer in remarkably high spirits.

I had, after all, deleted that godawful e-mail!

The clouds of doom had lifted. I saw sunshine! I saw rainbows! Oh, hell. I saw Skip Holmeier III.

There he was, toupee akimbo, scarfing down hors d'oeuvres from Cassie's tray.

I prayed that somehow he'd developed a mad crush on her in my absence, but that was not to be.

As if guided by radar, he turned around and spotted me instantly. And before you could say "Your toupee looks like Shredded Wheat," he was at my side.

"Jaine, my dear! I was hoping you'd be here. Let's find a secluded corner and chat. I've brought pictures of Miss Marple!"

For the first time I was grateful that Joy had roped me in as her indentured servant. It was the perfect excuse to keep Skip at bay.

"Sounds like oodles of fun, Skip, but I can't spend any time with you tonight. I'm afraid I'm on waitress duty."

With a feeble wave good-bye, I grabbed my tray from where I'd left it on the bar and zoomed off to the kitchen to load up on hors d'oeuvres.

When I came back out, Skip was over in a corner, talking with a very shaken Tonio.

Once more I wondered what Tonio had done to make Joy so angry.

And as it happened, Joy was about to get a whole lot angrier.

Because just then Alyce Winters, swathed in a bright

red spandex sheath, came slithering into the room, her raven extensions wriggling likes snakes on her shoulders.

She looked a hell of a lot tougher than the day I'd last seen her crying in the parking lot.

Strolling over to me, she plucked an hors d'oeuvre from my tray.

Nearby I could hear what sounded like a bull bellowing.

It was Joy, of course, her face almost as red as her dress.

Now she came roaring over to us.

"What the hell do you think you're doing here?" she hissed at Alyce. "I already told you. You're banned from the club."

"I spent my last ten thousand dollars on your worthless service," Alyce replied, not bothering to lower her voice. "The least I can get out of it is a crummy hors d'oeuvre."

She took a bite and wrinkled her nose in distaste.

"And I do mean crummy."

"Get out of here!" Joy sputtered. "This instant!"

The veins on her neck were throbbing, and in spite of Joy's attempt to keep her voice lowered, people were beginning to look.

"I want my ten thousand dollars back," Alyce said, not moving an inch.

"Over my dead body!" Joy hissed.

"Sounds like a plan," Alyce replied with a cool smile.

That did it. Alyce had pressed the right button. Now Joy was in fighting mode, swinging her arm back like she was going to slug Alyce Winters right in her nose job.

But after their set-to in the parking lot, Alyce knew what she was up against. Before Joy could make a move, Alyce reached out and grabbed Joy's wrist, then twisted it behind her back.

Joy winced in pain.

"You can't keep treating people the way you do, Joy. Not anymore. I'm going to put a stop to you."

Then she dropped Joy's wrist, turned on her heel, and walked out the door.

For once, Joy was at a loss for words. Was it my imagination, or did I see a flash of fear in her eyes? She stood there, rubbing her wrist, until she realized everyone was looking at her.

"Do forgive that ghastly intrusion," she said, piling on her British accent with a trowel. "A former member of the club. Mentally disturbed. Most distressing. But we mustn't let that upset us, must we? Let's party on!"

Then she faked her brightest smile and plunged back into the crowd, in full-tilt damage control mode.

Out from under her radarscope, I headed to the bar to thank Travis for helping me with Joy's password. And, not incidentally, to nab a wee sip of cheap champagne.

But when I got to the bar, Travis was nowhere in sight.

So I helped myself to the tiniest sip of Château Rite Aid, and thus fortified, continued making the rounds with my hors d'oeuvres—careful to avoid Skip, who had poor Tonio cornered, boring him senseless with anecdotes about his dearly departed Miss Marple.

By now I was starving. It had been ages since I'd wolfed down those two pot stickers at home (okay, four). I looked around the room and realized to my delight that Joy was nowhere in sight.

Hallelujah! I reached down for one of the hors d'oeuvres on my tray, a plump filo dough pastry bursting with cheese, and was about to pop it in my mouth when suddenly Joy came storming into the room, holding out her Godiva box.

"Who ate my chocolates?"

Her voice rattled the room like a sonic boom.

"Just a little while ago," she shrieked, "there were twelve chocolates in this box. And now there's only one!"

Omigosh. She was having another Godiva Meltdown!

She held up the empty Godiva box in one hand and the lone chocolate in the other.

"Who the hell ate my chocolates?" she screeched again.

Everyone just stared at her, too stunned to speak.

"Whoever did it," Joy said, her massive bosom heaving, "is blackballed from Dates of Joy for life!"

With that, she popped the lone chocolate in her mouth.

For a brief instant, I allowed myself to hope that this small dose of chocolate would calm her down and make her see that life was worth living. I know it always works that way for me.

But that, alas, was not to be.

Seconds after she swallowed it, she clutched her stomach and fell to the floor, writhing in pain.

People began screaming and reaching for their cell phones. Everywhere I looked, desperate singles were calling 911.

"Joy, sweetheart!" Tonio cried, racing to her side. "Are you okay?"

"Of course not, you idiot," Joy gasped.

As it turned out, those were her last words.

By the time the paramedics got there, Joy was dead.

Poisoned, as I would later learn, by a lethal dose of cyanide.

At long last, someone had taken the Joy out of dating.

YOU'VE GOT MAIL!

To: Jausten
From: Shoptillyoudrop
Subject: Arby's, Here We Come!

Would you believe Daddy forgot to make reservations at Le Chateaubriand? I only reminded him about 382 times. He insists he'll be able to get us a table. Oh, sure. At the last minute on Valentine's Day? Like that's ever going to happen!

Arby's, here we come.

XOXO,
Mom

To: Jausten
From: DaddyO
Subject: Oops!

With all the Sturm und Drang of dealing with Lester "The Gasbag Romeo" Pinkus, I forgot to make dinner reservations at Le Chateaubriand.

But fear not, Lambchop! I know how to grease a palm or two.

Love 'n' snuggles from
Your ever-resourceful,
Daddy

To: Jausten
From: Shoptillyoudrop
Subject: Worst Valentine's Ever!

Of course there weren't any tables available when we got
to Le Chateaubriand. I knew there wouldn't be. Daddy
tried to slip the maître d' some money to get us a table,
but the maître d' just flipped his quarter right back at him.

We were about to leave when Lydia Pinkus came running
up to us. She and Lester had a lovely table by the window,
and Lydia invited us to join them. I felt sort of funny about
it, after those two dozen roses from my "Secret Admirer,"
but Lydia insisted.

Daddy looked none too happy as we headed across the
room, but I made him promise to behave himself.

I was a fool to think he'd keep his word. He spent the
entire meal glaring at Lester and muttering under his
breath. When Lester made a harmless reference to his
days as an amateur boxer, Daddy began bragging about
his "grueling victories" on his college Ping-Pong team.

Worse, he took out his new Belgian Army Knife, the one I
was crazy enough to give him for Valentine's Day, and
kept talking about how the nose-hair trimmer could "kill a
man" under the right circumstances.

He insisted on using the built-in corkscrew to open our
bottle of wine and proceeded to shove the cork straight
into the bottle. We spent the whole night picking pieces of
cork off our tongues.

Daddy made a big show of giving me my Valentine's gift
at the table, which turned out to be a beautiful pink cubic
zirconia ring. (Daddy insists it's a diamond, but it sure
looked like CZ to me.)

"From your not-so-secret admirer," he said as he handed me the ring, giving Lester the evil eye.

Lydia, always gracious in any social situation, made a big fuss over my ring and tried to keep the conversation going, but it was tough sledding, what with Daddy shooting dirty looks at Lester every few seconds.

After a while, things got so tense that Lester excused himself and went to chat with Edna Lindstrom and Grace Vincent, who were sitting at a nearby table with some of the other Tampa Vistas gals. I only wished I were sitting there with them.

Eventually he came back, and I excused myself to go to the ladies' room. I'm afraid I may have had a wee bit too much wine (so much stress!) and it just raced right through me.

When I came back, I could see Lydia was at her wit's end, watching Daddy demonstrate the built-in callus remover on his Belgian Army Knife.

She excused herself and scooted off to the ladies' room. Everybody except Daddy was using any excuse in the book to get away from that awful dinner table. I myself was so upset, I couldn't eat a bite of the hot fudge sundae Daddy ordered for dessert. Well, okay, maybe I had a wee bit of ice cream. With a tad of fudge sauce. And maybe a few nuts. And a dollop of whipped cream. But that's all. I swear.

And wouldn't you know? I spilled fudge sauce on my brand new Georgie O. Armani jacket.

I swear, honey, it had to be the worst Valentine's ever!

Mom

To: Jausten
From: DaddyO
Subject: Bit of a Disappointment

Well, Lambchop, I must confess Valentine's Dinner was a bit of a disappointment. Your mom and I were forced to share a table with the Stinky Pinkuses—Lydia and her perfidious gasbag of a brother, Lester.

But I showed him a thing or two.

I'm sure he was impressed with the way I opened our wine bottle with my Belgian Army Knife. And I know I put the fear of God in him when I showed him the lethal power of my nose-hair trimmer.

The highlight of the evening, of course, was when I gave Mom her diamond ring. You should have seen Lydia's eyes bugging out. Lester's too. They were green with envy. And Lester could tell he didn't stand a chance with Mom.

Yes, I put the Gasbag Romeo in his place, all right.

Happy Valentine's Day to my little Lambchop
From her loving,
Daddy

To: Jausten
From: Shoptillyoudrop
Subject: Back to Normal

Daddy's strutting around, mumbling about how he put Lester Pinkus in his place, whatever that means. Oh, well. At least he seems to have given up the crazy notion that Lester has a crush on me. And so have I. Lester was nothing but a perfect gentleman at dinner. I can't believe he possibly sent me those flowers. It was probably just a mistaken delivery.

Thank heavens things can go back to normal.

Happy Valentine's Day, honey. Love you mucho.

XXX
Mom

To: Jausten
From: Shoptillyoudrop
Subject: Oh, No!

Horrible news, honey. I was just getting ready for bed when I realized my Valentine's ring is missing! I must have put it on the sink in the ladies' room at Le Chateaubriand when I washed my hands and forgot to put it back on again! I just called the restaurant, but no one has turned it in.

Worst of all, Daddy's convinced Lydia stole it!

Oh, dear. It's all too distressing.

Must get an Oreo—

XXX
Mom

To: Jausten
From: DaddyO
Subject: Diamond Thief!

Your mom's diamond ring is missing. And I know exactly
who took it. Lydia Pinkus! You should've seen her eyes
light up when she saw that thing. And she went to the
ladies' room right after your mom. No doubt she filched it
from where it was lying on the sink where your mom left it.
She and her no-goodnik brother are probably trying to sell
it on the black market at this very minute.

But fear not, Lambchop. The Pinkus's evil plot will be
foiled!

Love 'n' hugs from
Your crime-fighting,
Daddy

Chapter 10

It had been quite the Valentine's Day Crime Wave, n'est-ce pas?

First, Joy got bumped off. Then three thousand miles away, Mom's "diamond" ring disappeared into thin air. (Was it possible that Lydia Pinkus, model citizen and Tampa Vistas social doyenne, had stolen it?)

Of course, the shenanigans at Tampa Vistas paled in comparison to Joy's murder.

According to the *Los Angeles Times,* which I read the next morning as I scarfed down my cinnamon raisin bagel, Joy's final Godiva had been laced with cyanide. And according to Cassie, who'd overheard two cops talking when they came to cart the body away, whoever killed Joy had tossed the twelve missing chocolates out Joy's window into the alley below. Probably to make sure she ate the poisoned one right away.

A memorial service, the *Times* noted, was planned for later in the week.

Who on earth, I wondered, could have killed her?

Immediately I thought of Alyce, the client with a grudge. Hadn't she told Joy she was going to put a stop to her? Had she lived up to her threatening words with a poisoned chocolate?

And what about Tonio? Joy had been about to turn

him over to the authorities. Had Tonio killed her to shut her up?

I was pondering these questions, and whether or not I should nuke myself another bagel, when I heard Lance's familiar knock.

"Omigosh!" he cried when I let him in. "I just heard the news. What a tragic loss. I don't know how I'm going to cope."

"But you hardly knew her."

"Knew who?"

"Joy Amoroso."

"Joy? I wasn't talking about Joy. I was talking about the tanning parlor that closed over on Robertson Boulevard."

"That's a tragedy, all right. My heart breaks to think of all those poor, needy people running around West Hollywood without a tan."

"Scoff if you must. But if God wanted us to be pale, He would have never invented thong bikinis.

"So," he said, swiping the last bite of bagel from my plate. "What happened to Joy?"

"She's dead. Killed with a poisoned Godiva."

He rolled his eyes in disbelief.

"Please tell me you were nowhere near the scene of the crime."

"As a matter of fact, I was."

"Jaine, Jaine, Jaine!" he cried. "What is it with you? Everywhere you go, dead bodies seem to pop up."

It's true, I'm afraid. I've seen more than my fair share of corpses in my day. (All of which you can read about in the titles listed at the front of this book.)

"Do the police have any idea who did it?" Lance asked.

As it turned out, they did have a person in mind.

Namely, me.

* * *

Indeed, it was at that very moment that I heard a knock at my door. I opened it to find two men standing on my doorstep in ill-fitting suits, looking none too chirpy. One was a scrawny guy with an Adam's apple the size of a golf ball; the other, a beefier, refrigerator-sized chap with a military buzz cut.

"Are you Jaine Austen?" asked the Refrigerator.

I nodded, my throat suddenly dry.

"LAPD Homicide," the Refrigerator said as he and his partner flashed their badges. "May we come in?"

"Sure," I gulped, leading them inside.

"Guess I'd better be going," Lance said, jumping up from where he'd been sitting on my sofa.

He took my hands in his, a soulful look on his face.

"Remember, Jaine. I'm here for you whenever you need me. Except tonight. Donny and I are going to the movies. And tomorrow night we're hiking in Griffith Park. And Thursday we're having a picnic at the beach. Isn't that romantic?"

"Very," I said, icicles dripping from my voice.

"So if you need anything, anything at all, I'm thinking maybe you should call your parents."

And with those words of undying support, he went sailing out the door.

"Won't you sit down?" I said, turning to the detectives.

They plopped down on the sofa, still warm from Lance's tush.

"Can I get you anything?" I asked, hoping I could win them over with refreshments. "Juice? Coffee? Cinnamon raisin bagel?"

"Cinnamon raisin bagel?" The skinny detective looked interested.

"No, thank you," the Refrigerator replied, shooting his partner a stern look. "We never eat on the job."

From the looks of his gut, he sure was eating somewhere.

"Well, well!" said Detective Adam's Apple. "Isn't she a cutie!"

I smiled demurely until I realized he was talking about Prozac, who had wandered in from the bedroom and was now doing her version of a pole dance on the detective's ankles.

"Who do we have here?" he said, scooping Prozac up in his arms.

She looked up at him with wide green eyes.

Your future Significant Other, if you scratch me behind my ears.

The Refrigerator was having none of this little lovefest. He shot his partner a disapproving glare, then turned to me.

"We need to ask you a few questions about Joy Amoroso's murder."

"Ask away," I said, trying to look as non-homicidal as possible.

"It seems you were among those attending Ms. Amoroso's party," said Detective Adam's Apple, reluctantly abandoning Prozac to check his notebook.

"Yes, Joy called me at the last minute to help out at the party as one of the waitstaff."

"Apparently you decided to abandon your waitressing duties," the Refrigerator said, looking like he was ready to slap a pair of handcuffs on my wrists.

"Oh?" I replied, doing my best to maintain a look of wide-eyed innocence.

"We have a witness who says he saw you sneaking out of Ms. Amoroso's office."

Damn that Greg Stanton. What a blabbermouth.

"I misplaced my purse," I said, repeating the lie I'd told Greg, "and thought I'd left it there."

"You know, of course," said the Refrigerator, his eyes boring into mine, "that's where Ms. Amoroso's chocolates were located."

"Yes, I know. But I went nowhere near them."

He said nothing. Just continued to shoot me his laser glare.

"How would you describe your relationship with the deceased?" asked Detective Adam's Apple, trying to ignore Prozac, who had now draped herself across his legs.

"Businesslike. She hired me to write a brochure for her, as well as some online dating profiles. We were on perfectly cordial terms."

"Perfectly cordial?" The Fridge snorted. "Is that why you described her as a Psycho Cupid?"

Oh, hell.

"You found my brochure copy."

"It was right there," Detective Adam's Apple pointed out, "in Ms. Amoroso's recently deleted e-mail files."

"I had no idea," the Refrigerator added with a most unattractive smirk, "that Elmer Fudd was available for dating."

"Okay," I admitted. "So I didn't like Joy. But I swear, I didn't kill her."

The Refrigerator made a note on his pad.

I just hoped it wasn't a reminder to order an arrest warrant.

"Do you have any idea who did kill her?" he asked.

Reluctantly I told them about Alyce and the veiled threat she'd made at the party. I couldn't share my suspicions about Tonio, however, not without admitting I'd been crouching amid the dust bunnies under Joy's desk. Somehow I sensed they would not be favorably impressed.

"Well, thank you for your time," the Refrigerator said, hauling himself up from my sofa.

"Yes, thanks," Adam's Apple added, trying to extricate himself from Prozac's lingering embrace.

"I certainly hope I'm not a suspect."

If I'd been expecting reassurances, I was sadly disappointed.

"Just don't leave town," the Refrigerator said.

Ouch.

I ushered them both out and then leaned against the front door with a sigh.

"Dammit, Pro. They think I might have killed Joy. What am I gonna do?"

She looked up from where she was examining her privates.

What you always do in times of stress.

She knew me well.

Without missing a beat, I headed straight for the Oreos.

(It's in the genes.)

Chapter 11

Joy's memorial service was held at Westwood Mortuary, final resting place of mega-stars like Marilyn Monroe and Natalie Wood, who I'm sure were rolling over in their crypts at the thought of being saddled for all eternity with the Godiva Godzilla.

I wish I could say I showed up at the chapel to pay my respects and honor the dead, but the truth is I was hoping to run into someone who'd help me collect the money Joy owed me.

Lest you forget (I sure hadn't), I still hadn't been paid for all my hard work.

I was running late, and the rent-a-reverend conducting the service—a roly-poly man with round, rimless glasses—was in the middle of his eulogy when I showed up.

As I slid into a pew, I saw the place was practically empty. Just three mourners: Tonio, a blond woman a few rows in front of me, and a pungent guy in tattered clothing across the aisle.

The rent-a-rev had clearly never met Joy, because he was rambling on about what a swell gal she'd been. That he knew nothing about her was cemented by the fact that he kept calling her Joyce.

After winding down his highly fictional words of

praise, he peered out at us through his glasses and asked: "Is there anyone who'd like to say something?"

Across the aisle from me, the pungent fellow's hand shot up.

"I just wanna know," he asked. "Are there gonna be refreshments later?"

"No," replied the rent-a-rev. "I'm afraid not."

"Okay, then," he said. "I'm outta here." Sliding out from his pew, he confided to me, "Sometimes these memorial services put out a spread, you know? Oh, well. Off to the Church of the Good Shepherd. Maybe I'll have better luck there."

And with that, he ambled off to greener pastures.

"Er . . . is there anyone else who'd like to say something?" the minister asked when our hungry visitor had gone. "About the *deceased?*" he quickly added.

At which point the blond woman in front of me got up and headed for the podium.

There was something about her that looked awfully familiar. That thick blond pageboy. That chubby bod. Those tottering high heels.

When she turned to face us, I almost bust a gasket.

Holy mackerel! It was Joy! Back from Hell!

Even the devil didn't want her!

"Hello," the woman said. "I'm Joy's Aunt Faith."

I now saw that the woman was quite a bit older than Joy. But the resemblance was still uncanny.

She cleared her throat, a lacy white hankie balled up in her fist.

"I'll never forget the first time I saw little Joy," she said, her eyes glazed over at the memory. "She was only three years old, and her mother, my sister Eunice, had dressed her in her prettiest pink dress, with matching pink bows in her hair. They'd just moved out from Chicago, and my sister said to Joy, 'Say hello to your

Aunt Faith, darling.' And little Joy, in a gesture that would become all too familiar, hauled off and kicked me in the shin.

"Yes," she said with a grim smile, "Joy always was a rotten little kid, and she grew up to be an even more rotten adult."

"Excuse me, ma'am!" cried the rent-a-rev, jumping up from his seat behind the podium. "I'm not sure this is entirely appropriate."

"Hey!" She held out a warning hand. "You asked if anyone had anything to say about the deceased. I do, and I intend to say it."

"But, ma'am—"

"Forget it, buster. I'm not going to sit here and listen while you pretend my niece was anything but a miserable excuse for a human being."

Cowed by her no-nonsense attitude—not to mention her rather muscular upper arms—the rent-a-rev sank back down in his seat, and Aunt Faith continued her "eulogy."

"Joy took the matchmaking business her mother and I had built up over twenty years, and stole it right out from under our feet."

So Joy hadn't been lying when she said that matchmaking ran in her family.

"She drove my poor sister to her grave. But not me. I refused to let Joy's treachery ruin my life. Nope. I picked myself up and started my own jewelry business. *From Trash to Treasure*. One-of-a-kind baubles made from recycled bottle caps and typewriter parts."

She held out a bracelet made of typewriter keys and dangled it for our approval.

"In conclusion, I just want to say that wherever you are, Joy, I'm sure your chocolates are melting. Big time."

Her typewriter keys clanging, Aunt Faith stepped away from the podium and headed up the aisle, stopping at my pew.

"I've got some earrings that would look darling on you, hon," she said, handing me her business card. And with that, she tottered off.

So stunned was I by her performance, I barely listened as Tonio got up to the podium and talked about Joy. I caught a few phrases here and there . . . "a heart of gold" . . . "the love of my life" . . . "the world will be an empty place without her . . ."

Clearly he'd gotten his speech from the Hallmark School of Eulogies. And yet, if I wasn't mistaken, those were genuine tears I saw shimmering in his eyes.

Tonio returned to his chair, and the rent-a-rev, still reeling from Aunt Faith's "eulogy," stumbled back to the podium.

"Anyone else have something to say about the deceased?" he asked, looking at me. "Something *positive?*"

"Not a thing," I assured him.

"Well, then. I guess we're done here."

He wrapped up the service with the Twenty-Third Psalm and headed for Tonio with a mournful smile, assuring him that his beloved Joyce was safe in the sheltering arms of the Lord.

Tonio nodded blankly and then made his way up the aisle.

Today there was no trace of his usual lounge lizard good looks. His hair, normally slicked back to gelled perfection, had fallen into messy clumps. His spray tan had faded to a sickly orange. And his big brown bedroom eyes were puffy and red-rimmed.

Either he'd been up all night crying.

Or boozing.

I couldn't tell which.

I wasted no time following him out to the parking lot.

"Wait up, Tonio!" I called as he hurried to his car, a splashy silver BMW convertible.

"Oh, hello, Jaine," he said, catching sight of me. "Thanks so much for coming to pay your respects. I really appreciate it."

Geez. How was I going to tell him I was only there to see about my paycheck?

"Actually, Tonio, I said, a blush creeping up my face, "I came to ask you a favor. I never did get paid for the work I did for Joy, and I was wondering if you could help me get my money."

"How much did she owe you?"

"Three thousand dollars," I said, too embarrassed to mention the extra five hundred dollars she'd bribed me with to date Skip.

"Three grand?" Tonio snorted in disbelief. "Joy never paid writers that much. I'm sure she would've weaseled out of paying you the full amount."

Suddenly he realized he'd strayed quite a bit from eulogy mode.

"Not that she wasn't a wonderful person," he hastened to add. "Just sort of tight with a buck."

"Of course."

"But don't worry," he said, seeing the stricken look on my face. "I'll talk to her attorney and have him cut you a check for the full amount she promised you."

"Thanks so much, Tonio."

He was being so nice to me, I suddenly felt guilty about suspecting him of killing Joy. And yet I hadn't forgotten about that scene in her office. Sure as I'd been snorting dust bunnies, Joy had been threatening to turn Tonio over to the authorities.

"By the way, Tonio," I said, "I happened to overhear you and Joy talking the night of the murder."

"Oh?" His eyebrows lifted in surprise.

"Yes, Joy said something about turning you over to the authorities."

Those puffy eyes of his suddenly narrowed in suspicion.

"And just where did you hear all this?"

Oh, hell. I couldn't tell him I was hiding under Joy's desk, having just hacked into her e-mail account.

"I was out in the reception area," I fibbed, "and I heard you two talking in Joy's office. Joy, if I recall, was sort of angry."

"So she yelled at me. Big deal. What's it to you?"

Damn. Whatever goodwill I'd built had just gone sailing out the window.

"It's just that the police stopped by to question me," I said, putting on my tap shoes, "and I don't know what to tell them if they ask me about you. I mean, I can't lie and pretend I didn't hear anything. So I was hoping you could explain what Joy meant when she said she was going to turn you in to the authorities."

"Wait a minute. You don't think I killed her to shut her up, do you?"

"No, of course not," I lied. "But I'm afraid the cops might."

"That's crazy. For your information, Joy was threatening to report me to the DMV for driving without a license."

"That's all?"

"That's all. I failed the written test a couple of years ago. I kept getting a blinking red light confused with a yellow light. Anyhow, I never went back to take the test again."

"So you've been driving without a license all this time?"

"Yeah, and it drove Joy batty. I lied and told her I'd taken the test, and when she found out I hadn't, she went ballistic. You know how she could get."

Did I ever.

"So that's it. That was her big threat. She was a crazy lady, but I loved her. And I would never dream of hurting her."

And the tears welling in his eyes sure made it seem like he was telling the truth.

I was heading for my Corolla when a bright yellow VW Beetle came zooming into the parking lot and screeched to a halt in the spot next to mine.

Cassie sprang from the car, dressed head to toe in black leather, carrying a huge bouquet of dahlias.

"Did I miss the service?" she asked breathlessly.

"I'm afraid so."

"Damn, I had to drive to three different flower shops before I finally found these dahlias."

"How sweet of you, Cassie. They're beautiful."

"Joy hated dahlias," she said with a sly grin. "I think I'll go put them on her grave."

And off she went, skipping along toward the graveyard.

Melts your heart, doesn't it?

Chapter 12

"Seventeen dollars for a hamburger?!" I gasped, ogling the nosebleed expensive menu at Neiman Marcus's fanciest restaurant.

Lance had taken me there for lunch to cheer me up, knowing that I was a tad down in the dumps over my status as an Official Murder Suspect.

All around us were stick-thin fashionistas pushing food around their plates, resting their Manolos, and garnering the energy for another round of kamikaze shopping.

I feared the fashion police were standing by in the kitchen, just waiting to arrest me for showing up in my L.L. Bean turtleneck.

"Don't worry about the prices, hon," Lance said with an expansive wave. "I'm using my employee discount. Order whatever you want. As long as it's less than twenty bucks."

That wiped out about two-thirds of the menu, but luckily, my burger still qualified.

"Okay, I'll have the burger."

A look of horror crossed his face.

"At nine hundred ninety calories?"

"How do you know how many calories it has?"

"It says so right on the menu."

I looked down and saw that he was right. Underneath each item was a calorie count.

Talk about your guilt trips.

Well, it wasn't going to work on me. When it comes to calories, my motto has always been, "The more, the merrier." So when the waiter came to our table, I proudly ordered my burger, with *extra* ketchup.

Lance, after some severe tsk-tsking in my direction, ordered a sensible Mediterranean chopped salad (470 calories).

"I'm sorry I had to rush off the other day," he said when our waiter was gone. "But I'm here for you now, sweetie. You have to fill me in on what happened with the police. Don't leave out a single detail. Uncle Lance will hold your hand through this whole sordid ordeal."

He reached across the table and took my hand in his.

"Well—" I began.

But before I could make it to Syllable Two, he gushed, "Aren't they gorgeous?"

"Aren't what gorgeous?"

"My cuff links."

He flicked his wrists, flashing a pair of diamond-studded links on the French cuffs of his shirt.

"Donny gave them to me! On Valentine's night. He cooked me dinner at his place in the Hollywood Hills. Chateaubriand for two, a divine bottle of pinot noir, and chocolate mousse for dessert. He hid the cuff links in the mousse," he said, beaming like a lovesick puppy. "Isn't that the most romantic thing ever?"

"Not really. You could've broken a tooth."

"Go ahead," he said, patting my hand in a most patronizing manner. "Rain on my parade. I understand. You're frustrated and unhappy because I wound up with the heir to the Johnson & Johnson fortune and your significant other is a grumpy cat."

"Who says Donny's the heir to the Johnson & Johnson fortune?" I sniffed. "Did he tell you that?"

"No," Lance admitted, "but you should see his bathroom cupboard. It's stocked to the gills with Johnson & Johnson Baby Shampoo. It makes his hair silky soft," he added with a goofy grin.

"So the guy buys in bulk. That doesn't make him an heir."

"All I know is he's been showering me with gifts. First the Rolex. Then the cuff links."

"He does seem to have a lot of money," I conceded.

"It's not just about the money," Lance said, trying his best to look like he meant it. "Donny has all sorts of sterling qualities."

And he was off and running, singing the praises of his beloved Donny, how he was kind and caring and smart and funny, with impeccable taste in wine and clothing—and men, of course.

Eventually our food showed up, but that didn't stop Lance. He barely touched his Mediterranean salad as he blathered on about Donny.

I was sitting there, valiantly trying to keep my eyelids propped open, when I looked up and saw a slim, trendy guy with Brad Pitt aviator glasses walk into the restaurant. Wait a minute. I knew that guy. It was Travis, Joy's nerdy computer tech. Only he wasn't the least bit nerdy anymore. The former IT geek was duded up in an Italian suit, his floppy locks now artfully arranged in hip spikes.

Yikes. Talk about your makeovers. The guy had done a complete fashion U-ey.

"Excuse me just a minute." Somehow I managed to interrupt Lance, who was in the middle of describing Donny's eyes (cerulean blue with just a hint of aquamarine, for those of you taking notes). "I see someone I know."

"You actually know someone in this restaurant?" asked Lance, blinking in surprise.

"Yes, in fact, I do, and I'm going to say hello."

"Okay, but don't take too long. I still haven't told you about Donny's dimple."

I just prayed it was on his face.

I made my way to Travis's table, my L.L. Bean turtleneck and elastic waist pants attracting quite a few disapproving stares en route.

"Oh, hi, Jaine," Travis said when he saw me coming.

Up close, I could see he'd had his teeth whitened.

"Hey, Travis. How's it going?"

"Great. I just opened my new office. Here, have a card."

He took out a fancy silver card case and handed me an embossed business card, which read:

TRAVIS RICHARDSON
ELITE MATCHMAKING

"You've opened your own matchmaking service?" I asked.

"Yes. In fact, I'm meeting a client here for lunch."

Then he flashed me what I'd never seen at Dates of Joy: an appealing grin.

"You should drop by and see me."

"Sure," I nodded, still blown away by his transformation from geekster to sleekster.

After some rather wooden chat about what a shock Joy's death had been, I made my way back to Lance, who took up where he'd left off in his paean to Donny, rambling on until the check came.

"Thanks so much, Lance," I said as he paid the bill. "This was really very sweet of you."

"Oh, honey, what are friends for if not to be there for you in your time of need? Which reminds me, I never did hear about your horrible ordeal with the police. Where did all the time go?"

"Most of it, on Donny's dimple."

As we made our way out of the restaurant, we passed a tall blonde in a cashmere slacks set that probably cost more than my Corolla. She headed for Travis's table, undoubtedly the client he'd been talking about.

Looked like his new business was off to a booming start.

Picking up a mint from a bowl on the hostess stand (okay, three mints), I couldn't help but wonder if Travis's sudden change of fortune had anything to do with Joy's murder.

Back home, after an obligatory belly rub for Pro, I hurried to my computer and logged on to Travis's Web site. I checked out the dating profiles of the "typical clients" he'd used to lure in new members.

Holy mackerel. I recognized every one of them. Mainly because Travis had filched them all from Joy's database.

No wonder he was able to get his business off to such a fast start.

And just like that, Travis Richardson leapt on board my suspect list.

Was it possible the former geek had poisoned his boss from hell to get his hands on her client list?

Chapter 13

Much to my surprise, Elite Matchmaking was actually in a fairly elite part of town—just off South Beverly Drive in the heart of Beverly Hills.

I drove there the next morning, and after circling around the popular shopping area for what seemed like hours, I finally nabbed a parking spot and made my way to Travis's office.

I found it in a slightly run-down courtyard building, with loose bricks on the pathway and a fountain that had long since ceased to bubble. But with its vintage 1920s Spanish architecture, it had an undeniable charm.

After checking the directory, I made my way across the courtyard to Elite Matchmaking and knocked on the door.

"Come in!" Travis called out.

I turned the knob and stepped into his closet-sized office.

It was tiny to the max, but nicely decorated with a stylish area rug, sleek blond furniture, and three well-placed posters of happy couples holding hands and smiling adoringly at one another.

Travis sat behind his desk, dressed to the nines, with his spiky new hairdo and Brad Pitt aviators, his duct tape nerd glasses a relic of the past.

"Great to see you, Jaine! Have a seat."

He pointed to the only visitor's chair in the room, an Eames-ish number that picked up one of the colors in his area rug.

It took me all of two steps to reach it.

"So," he beamed, as I plopped down. "What do you think of my office?"

"It's great."

"My girlfriend decorated it. She's the one who picked out my new clothes, too."

"*You* have a girlfriend?" I blurted out.

Despite his new look, I still couldn't help thinking of him in geek mode.

"I mean, you have a *girlfriend!* How nice!"

"Actually I met her on Dates of Joy. She was one of Joy's few genuine clients."

"Joy fixed you up?"

"Are you kidding? Joy couldn't make a match if she signed up a hooker at a frat house."

He picked up a framed picture from his desk and showed it to me.

"Her name is Ellen. Isn't she pretty?"

"She's lovely," I said, staring down at a sweet-looking redhead with freckles and a slight overbite.

"I saw her picture on Joy's website and asked her out on the sly. Ellen was the one good thing I got from that rotten job."

"I wouldn't exactly say that, Travis."

"What do you mean?"

"I checked out your clients online, and they looked awfully familiar."

He had the good grace to blush.

"Okay, so I'm using Joy's database. I paid for those

profiles with two years of blood, sweat, and humiliation. Joy owed me."

"But you can't just take over her client list like that. Doesn't it belong to her heirs?"

"Not really. Joy's business wasn't incorporated. So technically, there's nothing to inherit. Besides, who'd even want it? Tonio needs a calculator to add two and two, and as far as I know all Joy's relatives are dead."

Clearly he'd never met Aunt Faith.

"And the fact is, I'm only using Joy's database to get started. Once I'm up and running, I'm going to dump the phony models and actors. I've already signed up a whole bunch of new clients from an ad I took out on Craigslist. "Which brings me to you, Jaine."

He whipped out a piece of paper and slid it across the desk. Glancing down, I saw that it was an Elite Matchmaking Membership Agreement.

"You know," he said, with that same appealing grin he'd flashed in Neiman's, "for only five hundred dollars I could set you up with a really nice guy. No Skip Holmeiers. I promise."

"Thanks, Travis, but that's about four hundred ninety-five more than I can afford right now."

"In that case," he said, snatching back the membership application, "why are you here?"

"Actually, I came to talk to you about Joy's murder. The police think I might have done it, and I'm trying to clear my name."

"You? A killer?" He threw back his head and laughed. "How ridiculous. You wouldn't have the nerve."

He was right, of course, but I was a tad insulted at his implication—hard to ignore—that I was about as fearless as a Teletubby.

"I happen to be a lot tougher than I look," I said, squaring my shoulders in my I MY CAT hoodie.

"Yeah, right," he smirked. "But you couldn't have killed Joy. Because I'm pretty sure I know who did."

"Who?"

"Greg Stanton."

"The artist? Really?"

"Absolutely," he nodded. "Joy had something on him. I'm sure of it. Something that kept him paying big bucks for her services year after year."

"You mean she was blackmailing him?"

"Big time."

Suddenly I remembered bumping into Greg outside Joy's office the night of the murder. At the time I was so worried about him ratting on me to Joy, it never occurred to me to wonder what *he* was doing there.

Greg may well have been the killer, but I couldn't ignore the hot suspect sitting right across from me. Joy had run roughshod over Travis for the past two years, and now after her death, he'd helped himself to her client list and a whole new life. He had more than enough motive for murder.

For all I knew, he'd been sneaking into her payroll and robbing her blind, saving up for the day when he could afford to open his spiffy new offices.

"By the way," I said as casually as I could, "I stopped by the bar to talk to you on the night of the murder, but you weren't there."

Guess I wasn't casual enough, because suddenly his face turned a most unsettling shade of red.

"What are you implying? That I had something to do with Joy's death? That I ran out to put that poisoned chocolate in her Godiva box?"

"No, not at all," I lied.

"Well, for your information, I left the bar for a few minutes to take a bathroom break. I may have been Joy's slave, but I think I was entitled to one of those."

"Of course," I said, with a placating smile, all the while wondering if I was sitting across the desk from Joy's killer.

Chapter 14

Working my magic charms (and doing a bit of groveling), I managed to smooth Travis's ruffled feathers and convinced him to give me contact information for several people on Joy's database I was eager to talk to.

First and foremost among them was Alyce Winters, the woman who'd threatened to "put a stop" to Joy less than an hour before she was murdered.

Soon I was tootling over to Alyce's apartment in West Hollywood—a sad stucco box of a building in desperate need of a paint job.

Like Alyce herself, it had seen better days.

Taking no chances that Alyce would turn me away at the intercom, I pressed several of the other buttons until someone buzzed me in. Then I rode up to Alyce's third-floor apartment in the building's creaky elevator, hoping the cables wouldn't snap en route.

Out in the hallway, I made my way along the threadbare carpeting to Alyce's place and rang her doorbell.

Seconds later a shadow darkened the peephole.

"Who is it?" Alyce sounded irritated.

"It's Jaine Austen. We met at Dates of Joy."

"What the hell do you want?"

"I need to talk to you. It's really very important."

I waited for what seemed like forever until at last I heard the sound of locks turning.

Finally the door swung open.

Alyce stood in the doorway, her skinny bod crammed into a leopard-skin jogging suit, jet black hair extensions hanging limply on her shoulders.

"I remember you," she said, staring out at me from an ashen face. "You worked for that bitch."

"Only temporarily," I assured her. "Honestly, I disliked Joy as much as you did."

"I hardly think that's possible."

She stood there, arms clamped tightly across her surgically enhanced chest, making no move whatsoever to invite me in.

"Well?" she said. "What's so damn important?"

Something told me she was not about to open up to me if she knew I was there to question her about the murder.

Time for a tiny fib.

"The *L.A. Times* has hired me to write a story about Joy. Ever since her death, rumors have been circulating about how unscrupulous she was, and they want to run an exposé on her."

At last, I saw a chink in Alyce's armor.

"That horrible woman!" she cried. "It's about time someone told the truth about her!"

Then a worried look crossed her brow.

"But I can't have my name in the paper. I'd die if anyone found out I'd been using a dating service."

"Not a problem," I assured her. "I'll quote you anonymously. Your name will never be published."

Not unless she turned out to be the killer, of course.

"Come on in," she said, her defenses finally down.

I followed her past a dimly lit foyer into a tiny living

room crammed to the gills with large-scale pieces of furniture—expensive items made for the wide open spaces of a Bel Air estate—not a one-bedroom apartment with a view of the Taco Bell across the street.

Off to the left a small kitchen was separated from the living room by a Formica breakfast bar.

"Coffee?" Alyce asked, heading for the kitchen.

"Sounds great."

She reached into her cupboard and pulled out a mug. After sloshing in some coffee, she turned to me and asked, "Milk? Sugar? Brandy?"

"Brandy?"

"Costco's finest," she assured me.

I watched as she added a generous slug to her own mug.

"Um, no thanks," I said, opting to stay sober for the time being.

"Your loss," she shrugged.

Then, with her coffee mug in one hand and the brandy bottle in the other, she led the way into the living room.

"God, what a nightmare it's been," she said, plopping down onto an oversized leather sectional. "I've been so stressed out, I haven't had my nails done in weeks. I tried press-on nails this morning, but one of the pinkies fell in the carpet and now I can't find it."

She held out her fingers, all but one pinky adorned in cherry red press-ons.

"Would you mind taking a look for it, hon?" she asked, adding some more brandy to her mug. "I'm exhausted."

And so the next few minutes found me on my knees, rooting around in her none-too-clean avocado shag carpeting. I unearthed a dime, a stale peanut, and an Extra-Strength Tylenol (which Alyce downed with her spiked coffee), but no pinky.

"Oh, there it is!" Alyce cried. "Under the coffee table."

She scrambled to her knees to pick it up.

"Damn. It's stuck to the carpet. Help me pull it out, would you? I don't want to break a nail."

I tried to pull out the damn pinky, but it was cemented there for life. Finally Alyce cut it out with manicure scissors, leaving a tiny bald spot in the carpet.

"There goes my security deposit," she groaned, eyeing the hole.

Then she added some more brandy to her coffee and took a deep slug.

"If one more thing goes wrong," she said, plopping back down on the sectional, "I may shoot myself. My life's been such a mess ever since Sonny died."

"Sonny?"

"My husband. A hedge fund manager. He lost his shirt in the market and was selling off all our assets to stay in the game. The stress of it all killed him. After I sold our house in Brentwood to pay off his debts, I barely had enough money to move into this dump."

"Then I took my last ten grand and signed up with Joy."

Lacing her coffee with more brandy, she took another gulp.

"I know it was a stupid thing to do, but she promised she'd set me up with a rich guy. And like a dope, I believed her. She wound up sending me on one lousy date with an insurance salesman from Downey."

"I remember. I was there when you confronted her that day in the parking lot."

"Can you believe how horribly she treated me?"

"It was awful," I agreed.

She added some more brandy to her coffee. By now it was probably all booze.

"And to make things worse, now the police suspect me of murder!"

At least I wasn't their only suspect.

"They say they have witnesses who saw me threatening Joy the night of the murder."

Through her alcoholic fog, she suddenly narrowed her eyes.

"Hey, wait a minute. You weren't one of those witnesses, were you?"

"Gosh, no," I managed to lie with a straight face.

The last thing I wanted was one of those press-on nails gouging my eyes out.

"When I said I was going to 'put a stop' to Joy, I didn't mean I was going to kill her. Although God knows I wanted to. I was only going to report her to the Better Business Bureau. "You believe me, don't you?"

She looked at me pleadingly with bloodshot eyes, and I have to admit I was swayed.

Either she was telling the truth or she was a damn good actress.

Then she looked down at her hands in dismay, remembering her press-on nail crisis. "Dammit! What am I going to do about this stupid pinky? Oh, well," she sighed. "I guess I'll just have to buy another set of nails."

By this point I'd had more than my share of her press-on saga. I really had to get in some serious questioning.

"I can't believe the police suspect you," I said, trying valiantly to wrench the topic back to the murder. "Do you have any idea who might have really killed Joy?"

"Anyone who ever met her."

A fat lot of help that was.

"Did you happen to see anyone go into her office on your way out of the party?"

"Hey, wait a minute." Alyce shot me a wary look. "I thought you were doing an exposé on Joy. Why all the questions about the murder?"

"Just gathering background," I said, channeling my inner Woodward and Bernstein. "Standard reportorial procedure."

"Oh. Okay."

Thank goodness, she bought it.

But before I had a chance to ply her with more questions, she jumped up from the sofa.

"Omigosh!" she cried. "With all the fuss over these damn nails, I forgot to give myself my insulin shot."

"Your insulin shot?"

"Yes, I'm a diabetic. Excuse me, hon. Gotta shoot myself up."

I watched in disbelief as she hurried down the hallway to her bathroom.

I'm no doctor, but I don't think diabetics are supposed to be guzzling brandy for lunch.

I was sitting there, wondering if I had time to snoop around her place for clues, when suddenly it hit me.

If Alyce was going to give herself an insulin shot, that meant she had access to syringes—exactly what she'd need if she wanted to inject a dose of cyanide into Joy's chocolate!

Sure enough, minutes later, she came back into the living room, tossing a used syringe into a wastepaper basket.

"There. That's done. Now where was I?"

At the top of my suspect list, that's where.

Chapter 15

The rest of my visit with Alyce was a total bust. I tried to get in a few questions about the murder, but all she cared about was trashing Joy and the shoddy quality of press-on nails. Finally, I gave her my card and urged her to call me if she remembered seeing anyone go into Joy's office the night of the murder.

By the time I got out of there, I was ready for a shot or two of that brandy myself.

Instead I drove home and nuked myself a jumbo cheese burrito I had sitting in my freezer. By now I was pretty darn hungry and stood hovering over the microwave as the plump burrito spun around, cheese oozing from its seams.

At last the countdown was over. The microwave dinged.

But just as I was reaching in to retrieve my cheesy treasure, there was a knock on my door.

With a sigh, I went to get it, afraid it was Lance hoping to mooch a free meal.

But it wasn't Lance. It was someone worse.

Much worse.

Standing on my doorstep was Skip Holmeier III. All spiffed up in a seersucker suit and polka dot tie (the latter coordinating quite nicely with his liver spots).

Oh, groan.

"Skip!" I forced a smile. "What brings you here?"

"Don't you remember? We have a date. We're supposed to have lunch today."

Yikes. I suddenly remembered that he had indeed called and asked me out. But that had been days before Joy died, and—bound by Joy's five-hundred-dollar bribe—I'd been forced into saying yes.

In all the hoo-ha of the murder, I'd forgotten all about it.

And now here he was, the world's least eligible bachelor, ready to take me to lunch.

"I hope we're still on," he said, with a pathetically eager smile.

I wracked my brain, frantically trying to think of a way out of this. Maybe I could tell him I was sick with the flu. Better yet, I'd tell him I'd contracted a tiny case of malaria. But then I saw that pathetic smile of his, and I just couldn't do it. The guy had driven all the way from Malibu (at twenty miles per hour, no doubt). It wouldn't kill me to have lunch with him, would it?

"Sure," I said. "We're still on. I'm just running a little late."

"That's wonderful!" he beamed. "I was afraid you were going to make up some lie and tell me you had the flu."

"Ha ha, what a crazy idea!"

"So how's my precious angel?" he asked.

"She's on the sofa, examining her privates."

Love light gleaming in his cataracts, he rushed over to my couch and swept Prozac up in his arms.

"You go get dressed," he said to me, kissing Prozac on the nose. "Prozac will keep me entertained. Won't you, darling?"

Wriggling uncomfortably in his arms, Prozac shot me a warning look.

Just FYI. He wears dentures. And they're loose.

I hurried off to get dressed, thinking longingly of my jumbo cheese burrito. Heaven only knew what kind of ghastly organic glop Skip would try to foist on me for lunch. I made up my mind that this time, no matter where Skip took me, I was going to order something decent to eat, preferably something with a side of fries.

After throwing on a pair of jeans and a cashmere sweater, I slapped on some lipstick, corralled my curls into a ponytail, and headed back out to the living room where Skip had Prozac trapped in his lap, gazing down at her like a lovesick teenager and making obnoxious kissy noises.

She glared up at me in high dudgeon.

If he pats my fanny one more time, I'm calling Gloria Allred.

Somehow I managed to drag him away from his beloved, and we headed outside to his mammoth Bentley.

"By the way," he said as we strapped ourselves in, "I thought it would be fun if I took you to meet Mother."

"We're having lunch with your mother?"

"She's dying to meet you," he nodded, inching out from the curb. "I've been telling her so much about you."

Good heavens. Skip was old enough to be my grandfather. His mother had to be pushing 100. Oh, well. At least with his mother at the table, there'd be no chance of him trying to play kneesies.

Soon we were on the road, Skip driving at a maddening twenty miles an hour. Which was bad enough on surface streets, but a nightmare on the freeway. People all around us were honking and cursing and giving us the finger, but Skip just kept on driving along, humming off-key, oblivious to the world.

Skip finally exited the freeway and was enraging the

drivers on surface streets when suddenly we came upon a vast expanse of green on our right.

I looked up and saw a large sign that informed me we had arrived at:

MALIBU HILLS CEMETERY

To my utter shock, Skip pulled in.

"What are we doing here?"

"Like I told you," he grinned, flashing his loose dentures. "We're meeting Mom."

Holy Moses! This nutcase was taking me to meet his dead mother!

He meandered along the cemetery's winding roads, then pulled into a parking spot and popped open the Bentley's trunk.

"I had my housekeeper pack us a nice organic picnic lunch," he said, hauling out a huge picnic basket.

Imagining the vegetarian nightmare lurking inside, I thought longingly of my jumbo burrito, oozing cheese.

Life can be so cruel sometimes, can't it?

With heavy steps, I followed Skip as he led me to an ornate headstone in a prized location under a shady elm tree. There he pulled out a blanket from the picnic basket and spread it out on the grass at the foot of his mother's headstone.

"Have a seat," he said, gesturing to the blanket.

I squatted on the itchy wool, feeling the cold ground beneath my jeans.

"Isn't this cozy?" Skip asked.

"Very," I said, watching some grave diggers prepping a final resting place in the distance.

"Hi, Mom!" he chirped to his mother's headstone. "I brought Jaine!"

Then he turned to me.

"Mom says hello."

"That's nice."

"Don't you want to say hello back?"

Oh, hell. He expected me to talk to her!

"Er . . . hello, Mrs. Holmeier," I said, forcing myself to talk to the headstone.

"Mom says no formalities around here. Her name is Miriam."

"Hello, Miriam."

"But she likes to be called Mimsy."

I forced a smile and said, "Hello, Mimsy."

"So what do you think, Mom?" Skip asked his dead mother. "Isn't she a peach?"

He cocked an ear, listening to Mimsy from beyond the grave.

"She says you're very sweet."

"How nice."

He looked at me expectantly. Dammit. He was waiting for me to talk to her again.

"Er . . . thank you, Mimsy," I said, shooting the headstone a dopey grin.

"Well," Skip said, "now that you've met Mom, it's time you said hello to Miss Marple."

"Miss Marple's here, too??"

"She sure is. Check out the headstone next to Mom's."

I looked at the neighboring headstone, and sure enough, it read:

JANE MARPLE HOLMEIER
BELOVED COMPANION TO SKIP HOLMEIER
"OUR LOVE IS HERE TO STAY"

I gawked at it in disbelief.

"But you're not allowed to bury pets in a human cemetery."

"You pay the right people enough money," he said with a wink, "and you can do anything. Anyhow, Miss Marple asks if you'd mind moving just a tad. You're sitting on her tail."

I jumped up, as if I really had been sitting on her tail.

The guy had me practically believing this nonsense.

"So what do you think of my Jaine, Miss Marple?" He cocked his ear toward Miss Marple's grave. "Omigosh!" he said, turning to me. "Can you hear that?"

"Hear what?"

"She's purring. That means she really likes you."

And on that good news, he grinned and said, "Let's eat!"

Smacking his lips, he opened the picnic basket and started taking out our lunch from culinary hell: pieces of cardboard posing as crackers, slabs of rubber posing as nonfat cheese, and a viscous white glob of what turned out to be goat yogurt, topped with sunflower seeds.

To wash it all down, he broke out a bottle of vintage celery tonic.

Somewhere in my mouth, my taste buds were playing taps.

And then a miracle happened. Skip reached into the basket and took out a humungous sandwich on a plate, covered with saran wrap.

"What's that?" I asked, my taste buds suddenly jolted awake.

"Egg salad sandwich with bacon," Skip replied.

"Looks dee-lish," I said, reaching for the plate. "Don't mind if I have a bite."

"Oh, no!" he said, snatching the plate away from me. "The sandwich is for Mom. It's her favorite. All this cholesterol is what put her in her grave. It can't hurt her now, though," he said, laying the plate at the base of the gravestone.

"You think she'd mind if I took a tiny bite?" I asked.

"No, not at all. But I would," he said, swatting away my hand. "I can't have you clogging your arteries with cholesterol."

I can't tell you what torture it was sitting there, gnawing at those cardboard crackers and rubber cheese, Mimsy's egg salad sandwich just inches from my grasp. It was all I could do not to leap over and nab it.

But somehow I refrained.

The meal flew by in a volley of questions from Mimsy and Miss Marple—as relayed by Skip—about my education, my hobbies, my background, as well as my favorite authors, movies, and cat foods.

Apparently I passed the test.

"They both love you!" Skip exclaimed, toasting me with his celery tonic. "Which means our relationship can go on to the next phase."

That phase, as far as I was concerned, was called "Over."

No way was I going out with this guy again. I had to cut things off right here and now, and tell him I simply wasn't interested.

"Look, Skip, I have something to say."

"Me, first," he said like an eager puppy. "I just want to say thank you. This has been the happiest day I can remember in years."

His cataracts misted over with tears.

I looked down at his frail, liver-spotted hands, and suddenly I was overwhelmed with pity for this loony old coot. It was the happiest day he'd had in years, and I wasn't about to ruin it. Today would be my gift to him.

"So what did you want to say?" he asked.

"Um . . . pass the yogurt?"

Skip was on such a high going home, he hit the pedal to the metal, sending the speedometer zooming all the way to thirty miles an hour. He chattered happily about how much fun we were going to have together, sailing his yacht to Majorca, getting season tickets for the ballet, and spending Christmas at his ski lodge in Aspen.

It was actually beginning to sound pretty good, until I remembered I'd be doing all this jet setting with Skip and his celery tonic glued to my side.

No, I'd definitely have to break up with him. As soon as I thought of a way to let him down gently.

Centuries later (okay, it was an hour and thirty-two and a half minutes), he dropped me off at my duplex, promising to call soon.

I waved good-bye and waited a small eternity until he'd driven off. Then, without any further ado, I dashed into my apartment, where I had my long-awaited tryst with my jumbo burrito.

I spent the rest of the day holed up with a *Real Housewives of Beverly Hills* marathon, recuperating from my coffee klatch with the dead.

When I'd finally had my fill of catfights in Louboutins, I looked up Skip's address on WhitePages.com and then sat down and wrote him a lovely note explaining that I could no longer see him, due to the fact that he was a certified loonybird.

Okay, so I didn't really call him a loonybird. Instead, I wrote something about irreconcilable differences and how it was best we not date for the next millennium or two. I signed it with a heartfelt frowny face, threw a raincoat over my chenille bathrobe and headed to my corner mailbox, where it was with the utmost sense of relief that I tossed the letter into the slot.

I walked back to my apartment with a spring in my step, a song in my heart, and a jumbo blueberry muffin in my hands. (Compliments of a pit stop at my corner Starbucks.)

At long last, I was Skip-free.

Chapter 16

The next morning I decided to pay a little visit to Travis's number one suspect—Greg Stanton.

Travis had said he was sure Joy had blackmailed Greg into joining Dates of Joy.

It sure made sense to me. From the moment I saw him cuddled up with that brunet beauty at Simon's Steak House, I could not for the life of me figure out why a guy like Greg would need Joy's services.

I looked up his address on Travis's handy dandy contact list and, after slipping into some sweats and a hoodie, was soon zipping off to his house in the ultra-tony North of Montana section of Santa Monica, where unassuming little cottages sell for upwards of two mil.

Greg's house, however, was anything but unassuming. A massive Mediterranean-style McMansion surrounded by lush foliage, it was dotted with so many balconies, I almost expected to see either Rapunzel or the Pope pop out on one of them.

A Lamborghini parked in the driveway allowed me to hope that Greg was home.

After parking my lowly Corolla at the curb, I trotted up the path to Greg's massive front door and rang the bell.

Inside I could hear chimes reverberating, and seconds

later, much to my delight, Greg answered the door himself—in jeans and a work shirt, his surfer blond hair glinting in the morning sun.

Thank heavens I wouldn't have to talk my way past a servant.

"Hi, Mr. Stanton!" I chirped in my cheeriest voice. "I don't know if you remember me. I was working for Joy Amoroso when she died."

"I remember you, all right. What the hell do you want?"

Okay, so what he really said was, "How can I help you?"

But I could tell by the look on his face he was none too thrilled to see me.

Sensing I wouldn't make it past the front door if he knew I was there to grill him about the murder, I decided to stick with my *L.A. Times* exposé ruse.

"Actually, I'm writing an exposé on Joy for the *L.A. Times*. All about her unscrupulous business tactics."

"The *L.A. Times* wants *you* to write a story?" he asked, blinking in surprise. "Aren't you one of the murder suspects?"

"Me? A suspect?" I said, trying to keep my voice light and airy. "That's the first I've heard of it."

"According to the police, you were seen coming out of Joy's office the night of the murder."

Probably because you told them, blabbermouth.

"They seemed to believe me when I explained that I just popped in to look for my purse. And that's why I was there, Greg. Just looking for my purse."

He raised a skeptical brow.

"So how about it?" I persisted. "Can you spare a few minutes for an exposé on Joy?"

If I'd expected him to jump at the chance to trash Joy, I was sadly mistaken.

"I doubt I can be any help to you," he said stiffly. "My dealings with Joy were always quite amicable."

Spoken with all the heartfelt sincerity of a press agent.

"That's great!" I said, forcing a smile. "I need to get both sides of the story. It would be wonderful to be able to quote someone who actually had a good experience with her."

"Wish I could help," he said, starting to close the door, "but I'm just finishing up my latest painting. I've got to get back upstairs to my studio."

"It won't take long, I promise."

Maybe it was my winsome smile. Or the pleading look in my eye. Or perhaps my foot wedged on his doorstep.

Whatever the reason, he changed his mind.

"Oh, okay," he said, waving me inside with a sigh.

I followed him to a huge living room, tastefully decorated in various shades of brown and taupe. All the pieces looked expensive; none of them exciting. It was like walking into a hotel lobby. The only spot of color was a red box of Valentine's chocolates on the coffee table.

How odd. I remembered Joy telling me Greg painted "fabulously colorful landscapes." So why was a guy who made his living working with color living in a symphony of beige?

"Have a seat," he said, ushering me to one of two beige sofas flanking the coffee table.

He sat down across from me, perched at the edge of his sofa cushion, his hands on his knees, clearly ready to cut the interview short the minute he could.

I eyed the box of chocolates on the coffee table, but he made no move to offer me one.

First Joy, now Greg. There certainly was a lot of choco-hoarding going around.

"So what would you like to know?" he asked.

"Were you aware of any of Joy's shady dealings? How she used phony pictures of models and actors to lure clients? How once she had her clients roped in, she rarely came through with a match?"

"I'd heard rumors," he admitted, "but she was always up front with me. The minute I signed with her, she started setting me up with great women. She really was the best in her business," he said, smiling a smile that didn't quite ring true.

"Do you mind my asking why a handsome guy like you needed a matchmaking service?"

"You wouldn't believe how many women are only interested in me because I'm a famous artist," he said, raking his fingers through his mop of sun-bleached hair.

I'd bet my bottom Pop-Tarts there'd be hordes of women eager to run their hands through that mop— with or without a famous artist attached.

"I needed Joy to find me someone who'd love me for myself."

"How long were you with her?" I asked.

"About five years."

"That long, huh? Funny that someone who was the best in her business couldn't make a match for you in five years."

Anger flashed in his eyes for the briefest beat; then he forced a smile.

"Love's not easy," he shrugged.

"So you don't agree with the scuttlebutt that she cheated her clients, even blackmailing some of them?"

I waited for a reaction to my blackmail bait, but he wasn't biting.

"I don't know how she treated anybody else," he

said, "but she was always wonderful to me. I'm really going to miss her," he added, doing his best to strike a mournful pose.

As he sat there in his work shirt and jeans, his hands clasping his knees, something about his appearance didn't ring true.

And then it hit me.

It was his hands. They were perfectly clean. Not a spot of paint anywhere.

If he'd just been working on a painting, as he'd claimed, shouldn't his hands be splattered with paint?

"Well," he said, getting up, "I've really got to get back upstairs to work."

Doing what? I wondered.

And as I followed him to the front door, I noticed something else that seemed odd. Looking down at the socks peeking out from his running shoes, I saw that one of them was blue, and the other brown.

Had he gotten dressed in a hurry? Or was this some sort of artistic fashion statement?

It wasn't until I was back outside strapping myself in my Corolla that I came up with another explanation for those mismatched socks.

Was it possible that one of the area's leading artists, famous for his use of color, was actually colorblind?

But that simply couldn't be.

Or could it?

I drove to the end of the block and waited about five minutes. Then I headed back to Greg's McMansion. Something fishy was going on with that guy, and I was determined to find out what it was. Crouching along the rosebushes out front, I made my way to the side of the house, then tiptoed toward the back, checking each room for signs of Greg. But he was nowhere to be seen.

Then I remembered that he said his studio was upstairs.

By now I was at the back of the house. I looked up and saw a room with large floor-to-ceiling windows and French doors leading out to a balcony. The perfect space for a studio.

But how was I supposed to spy on Greg if he was up on the second floor?

And then I spotted it. The answer to my prayers: A large oak tree, several of its branches practically touching the room's balcony.

Somehow I had to climb that tree.

The last time I'd shimmied up a tree was never, but I had to give it a shot.

It wasn't easy, but with strength, determination, and a small ladder I found propped up against Greg's garage, I managed to scramble up to a branch with a view of the room.

The branch looked strong. But was it strong enough to hold me and the cavalcade of calories camping on my thighs?

Gingerly I inched out along the branch, holding on to a crevice in the tree trunk, just in case the branch gave way.

Thank heavens the mighty oak remained mighty, and the branch held firm.

If I craned my neck just a tad, I could see directly into what was indeed Greg's studio.

An empty easel was set up in the corner of the room, a palette of oils resting on a nearby stand. Everything was spotless. No mess. No blobs of spattered paint anywhere. Just the empty easel, the palette, and a few blank canvases propped against the wall.

If Greg had been working on a painting, where the heck was it?

Just then, the door to what looked like a closet in the

corner of the room opened, and Greg came out carrying a canvas. A colorful landscape of a country lane. So vibrant and alive, everything the rest of his house wasn't.

He propped it up on the easel and then took out a dust rag from his pocket and began dusting it off.

Huh?

Who the heck dusts off an oil they've just finished painting? Obviously this picture had been sitting in that closet for quite some time.

And then, much to my amazement, he started dusting his palette of oils. The globs of paint were hard as a rock. The darn thing was a prop!

Curiouser and curiouser, to quote my good buddy L. G. Carroll.

Thoroughly flabbergasted, I watched as Greg took out his cell phone and started making a call.

The French doors to his balcony were open and, leaning forward, I strained to hear what he was saying.

"Hello, Calista?" His voice filtered out from the studio. "It's Greg. The paint's just dry on my latest painting." He flicked the dust rag over the canvas. "I think it's one of my best. Hoping we can get at least a hundred grand for it . . . Okay, I'll bring it right over."

He clicked off the phone, and then, much to my dismay, he started for the balcony.

Oh, hell. He was coming to close the French doors!

Frantically, I scooted back to the tree trunk. I got there just in time to hear the doors lock. I only hoped he hadn't seen me.

Peering out between the leaves, I watched as Greg headed out the studio door, the canvas tucked under his arm.

And suddenly everything clicked into place. Greg had no paint on his hands because he wasn't a painter. He was no more an artist than I was. Somewhere someone else was doing the actual painting, and Greg was taking all the credit. Greg Stanton was a colorblind fake! That was his dirty little secret. Somehow Joy found out about it and had been blackmailing him all these years.

Maybe Greg had finally put an end to her extortion with a poisoned chocolate.

Perhaps one from the very box I'd seen on his coffee table.

I sat there, feeling quite proud of my deductive powers. Not to mention my tree-climbing skills.

And that's when the squirrels attacked.

Yes, I was up in that old oak tree, feeling quite Sherlock Holmesian, when suddenly I looked down and saw two rather perturbed squirrels squealing at the base of the tree, their furry tails swishing in ire.

For purposes of this narration, I shall call them Rocky and Bullwinkle.

What on earth were they so angry about?

And then I realized that crevice I'd been using to keep a grip on the tree was their little home, their pied-à-terre, their Casa De Acorns. I felt around inside and sure enough, there were a whole bunch of nuts stored inside.

No wonder they were so angry. I had invaded their stash!

In the distance, I could hear the sounds of a car door slam and an engine rev. Probably Greg, driving off to sell his painting.

Meanwhile, the squirrels were hurtling up the tree, fury in their beady little eyes.

"I come in peace!" I cried. "Honest, fellas. I don't even like acorns!"

Somehow they were not mollified.

One of them, I believe it was Rocky, was baring his teeth in a most frightening manner.

Any minute now he'd be sinking those teeth into my fanny, and I'd be spending the next several hours in an emergency room getting a series of painful rabies shots.

Frantically I pulled off my sneaker and shooed Rocky away as I shimmied down the tree. It seemed like centuries, but at last I reached the ladder and clambered the rest of the way down.

Never had I been so relieved to be on terra firma.

Just when I thought I was home free, however, I felt something around my ankle. Oh, hell. It was Rocky, chomping down on my pant leg.

"I swear, I don't have any of your nuts!" I cried. "Now let me go!"

But Rocky was not about to let go. And now I saw Bullwinkle charging down the tree and aiming for my other leg. I had no choice but to step out of my sweats and let the squirrels have them.

Unbelievable! Why, just last Christmas a pair of Dobermans had ripped my favorite Eileen Fisher outfit off my back at a holiday party (a ghastly episode you can read all about in *Secret Santa*, now available in all the usual places). And here I was, being undressed all over again by a pair of squirrels.

All I can say is it's pretty pathetic when the only males interested in tearing off my clothes have four legs and tails.

But I digress.

Rocky was now zipping up the tree, chirping in victory, my sweatpants trailing behind him. Bullwinkle, meanwhile, shot me what looked suspiciously like a smirk and then scooted up behind his buddy.

Oh, well. At least I wouldn't need those rabies shots.

I started for my car, dying to get home and soak in the tub for the next forty-seven hours, when suddenly I realized my car keys were in my pants pocket!

Damn! Back I went to that dratted oak tree where Rocky and Bullwinkle were now chewing on my sweats, no doubt looking for the emergency M&M's I keep in the pockets.

I climbed the ladder and reached for a pant leg that was dangling from a branch. I gave it a yank, but for such little critters, Rocky and Bullwinkle were surprisingly strong. They clung to my pants with their sharp little teeth, not giving an inch.

Frantically I stood there yanking at my pants, praying that my rodent buddies would not come charging down at me.

At last my car keys come clattering to the ground, and I picked them up and headed for my car.

The last I saw of Rocky and Bullwinkle, they were noshing on my M&M's.

Chapter 17

People think California is the land of sunshine, but it can get quite frosty here in February and March, especially if you're not wearing pants.

I drove home with the car heater on, vowing to never again get in a tiff with a pair of squirrels.

They may look cute, but trust me, they don't fight fair.

At last I arrived at my duplex and was heading up the front path to my apartment, practically naked from the waist down, my thighs on view for all the world to see, when I looked up and saw someone at my front door.

Oh, hell. It was one of the homicide detectives. The skinny one with the Adam's apple.

"Hello, Ms. Austen," he said, making a valiant effort not to stare at my thighs, which by now were sprouting goose bumps the size of popcorn.

"Excuse the way I look," I managed to say. "I . . . um . . . lost my pants."

"So I see."

"Yes, I gave them to a needy homeless person."

"How generous of you," he said, shooting me a dubious look. Then he cleared his throat, getting down to business. "I need to talk to you."

Uh-oh. I didn't like the sound of that.

At which point, his phone rang. He snapped it open, saying, "Detective Willis here."

So that's what his name was. I had to remember not to call him Detective Adam's Apple.

"Got it," he was saying. "I'll be right over."

"Sorry," he said to me, flipping his phone shut. "I've got to go. Emergency. Why don't I stop by tomorrow for a little chat. Say, nine a.m.?"

"Of course," I said, and I headed for my apartment with as much dignity as a woman without any pants can muster.

The minute I got inside, I headed straight for the bathtub.

Normally, soaking in a steamy hot bubble bath relaxes me, but not that day. I lay there up to my neck in strawberry-scented bubbles, a mass of raw nerve endings, haunted by the memory of Rocky and Bullwinkle charging after me with bloodlust in their eyes.

I cringed to think what a sniveling weakling I'd been in front of a pair of fuzzy-tailed rodents. No doubt about it. I was a disgrace to part-time semiprofessional private eyes everywhere.

And then, as if being terrorized by a pair of squirrels weren't enough, I had to endure the humiliation of Detective Adam's Apple seeing me sashaying up my front path without any pants! If only I'd worked on toning my thighs more often. Or ever.

And why on earth did Detective Adam's Apple want to talk to me? What if the police had narrowed down their suspects and decided I was the killer? What if Detective Adam's Apple had shown up to arrest me for Joy's murder?

But that couldn't be. If they were going to arrest me,

they would've sent a bunch of cops and hauled me away then and there.

I sank back in the tub, relief flooding my body. I was in the clear, after all.

But wait! I thought, jolting back up again. What if they *wanted* to arrest me but didn't have enough evidence, and Detective Adam's Apple had dropped by for a casual chat, hoping I'd say something that would nail me as the killer?

But I *wasn't* the killer, I reminded myself, sliding back down in the tub. I was perfectly safe. All I had to do was tell the truth—that although I happened to be in Joy's office that night, hacking into her computer and hiding under her desk with dust bunnies the size of Chihuahuas, I was as innocent as a babe in swaddling clothes. Surely they'd have to believe me.

But wait! I jolted back up. Even if they let me go on murder charges, what if they convicted me of computer hacking? How many years would I spend in jail for that?

By now I practically had whiplash from jerking up and down in the tub so much.

I was sitting there, picturing myself sharing a jail cell with a gal named Big Mike, looking back on my adventure with Rocky and Bullwinkle as a carefree romp in the wine country, when I heard a loud banging on my front door.

"Jaine!" I heard Lance calling out. "It's me."

I hauled myself out of the tub and into my chenille bathrobe, then hurried to let him in, leaving a trail of damp footprints in my wake.

"Guess what, Jaine?" he said, rushing into my apartment, all spiffed up in his Neiman Marcus work togs. "The Town Crier just called. She said she saw you talking with some guy in front of your apartment, half naked!"

The Town Crier to whom Lance referred was our neighbor across the street, Helen Hurlbutt, a woman who's never met a rumor she hasn't felt the urge to spread.

"So? What's it all about?" Lance asked, plopping down onto my sofa, wide-eyed with anticipation.

With a weary sigh, I launched into my saga, telling him how I climbed a tree to spy on Greg Stanton only to be terrorized by a pair of pant-stealing squirrels and then came home to find Detective Adam's Apple who was coming back to talk to me tomorrow, the very thought of which had me terrified I was going to be arrested for Joy Amoroso's murder.

Lance sat there for a beat, slack jawed.

When at last he'd taken it all in, he said: "*You* climbed a *tree?* The woman who gets winded brushing her teeth?"

"Let's focus here, Lance. The bottom line of this story is that I may be trotting off to jail for a murder I didn't commit."

"Don't be absurd, Jaine," he said with a careless wave. "You can't possibly be arrested for murder. You're not the killer."

Spoken with an air of such authority that I suddenly found myself soothed to my very core.

"Then again," he said, scratching his blond curls, "I just read a story in the paper about some poor guy who was arrested for a murder he didn't commit and spent thirty years festering in jail until they realized he was innocent all along."

Yikes. So much for soothed.

"But, hey," he said, seeing the stricken look on my face. "That's never going to happen to you. I'm a hundred percent positive. Well, eighty-six percent, anyway. Fifty-two percent in a worst-case scenario."

"What a relief. I can sleep easy now."

My sarcasm went winging over his blond curls.

"Whatever you do, wear something nice for your interrogation tomorrow. Studies show that well-dressed felons are five times more likely to be acquitted than those dressed like slobs. Just remember—no elastic waist pants!"

Good heavens. Why does everything with that man always boil down to elastic waist pants?

"And if worse comes to worst, I'll get you the best defense attorney Donny's money can buy. Speaking of Donny," he added, his eyes lighting up, "look at the fabulous tie he just bought me!" He flapped one of Hugo Boss's finest in my face. "Isn't it divine?"

"Just divine," I muttered. "Maybe he can get me some cute designer prison wear."

Once again, my sarcasm sailed up into the ozone.

"Gotta run, sweetie," Lance said, wrapping me in a hug, "or I'll be late for work. "So glad I could cheer you up!" he cried as he raced out the door.

And that's the crazy thing. He actually thought he'd cheered me up.

Oh, well. There was only one way I was going to get through all this: Hang tough, be strong, and head for the Oreos.

YOU'VE GOT MAIL!

To: Jausten
From: Shoptillyoudrop
Subject: On the Warpath

Daddy's been on the warpath, convinced that Lydia Pinkus stole my diamond ring and is working in cahoots with Lester to sell it on the black market. Did you ever hear anything so absurd? He refuses to accept the fact that someone else might have taken it from the ladies' room at Le Chateaubriand, or that it fell into the wastebasket and was tossed out by accident. No, he's certain that Lydia and Lester—or, as he calls them, The Evil Axis—are responsible.

Of course, Daddy has had it in for Lydia ever since I can remember. Over the years he's suspected the poor woman of everything from petty theft to murder. Do you remember last year, when he was certain she'd killed Irma, her childhood friend from Minnesota, and was hiding her chopped-up body in her refrigerator? I tell you, when it comes to Lydia, your father's imagination knows no bounds.

Now he insists that Lydia and Lester have my ring stashed away somewhere, and he's determined to get it back. Oh, dear. I just hope he doesn't try to break into Lydia's townhouse like he did last year when he was searching for Irma's body.

I've told him if he takes one step near that townhouse without Lydia's permission, I'm filing for divorce. He's promised to behave.

XOXO,
Mom

To: Jausten
From: DaddyO

Can't write much now, Lambchop. Busy working on my plan to tunnel my way into Lydia's townhouse. Must run to Home Depot to buy a shovel.

Love 'n' hugs,
Daddy

To: Jausten
From: DaddyO
Subject: Cancel That Shovel

Wonderful news, Lambchop! It looks like I won't have to tunnel my way into Stinky Pinkus's townhouse, after all. Lydia's throwing a party and has invited the neighbors for a slide show presentation of The Gasbag's recent trip to Nepal. What a snore fest that's going to be. But luckily, I won't be around to see it. When they dim the lights, I plan to sneak out and conduct a thorough search of the premises.

Somewhere in that den of iniquity I know I'll find your mother's diamond ring. I just hope I get there before The Evil Axis has sold it on the black market.

Love 'n' snuggles from
Your Crime-fighting,
Daddy

To: Jausten
From: Shoptillyoudrop
Subject: Come to His Senses

Lydia's just called. She's invited us over to see slides from Lester's recent trip to Nepal. (That man has led such an interesting life!)

I thought for sure Daddy would make a big fuss about going. But on the contrary, he seems quite enthused. Says he's always wanted to learn more about Nepal. He even apologized for his accusations against Lydia and Lester. Says he was wrong to think they'd stolen my ring, that he jumped to a foolish conclusion.

Thank heavens, he's come to his senses.

XOXO,
Mom

To: Jausten
From: DaddyO

Dearest Lambchop—Did I tell you my Belgian Army Knife comes with a miniature crowbar? Perfect for jimmying open Stinky Pinkus's locked drawers!

Chapter 18

Ibarely slept a wink that night, tossing and turning and dreaming I was being chased by a squirrel with a machete.

The next morning I woke up drenched in sweat, Prozac clawing at my chest for her breakfast.

With a pained moan, I staggered to the kitchen.

"I'm a fool to be worried about going to jail, aren't I, Pro?" I asked, desperate for reassurance.

She looked up at me with big green eyes that could mean only one thing.

Minced Mackerel Guts again? How come I never get any steak tartare?

Somehow I managed to force down my own breakfast. I was so nervous, I could barely finish my second cinnamon raisin bagel.

Checking my e-mails, I shuddered to read about Daddy's plan to "search the premises" of Lydia Pinkus's town house. But I couldn't waste time worrying about Daddy. Not with Detective Adam's Apple on his way over.

Desperate to make a good impression, I dressed with care, choosing fresh-from-the-cleaners khaki pants, brown suede boots, and a simple black silk pullover sweater.

Then I blew out my mop of curls and slapped on some makeup, checking every few minutes to make sure I hadn't forgotten to put on my pants.

I still had about fifteen minutes till my nine a.m. appointment, so I wisely used the time to straighten my apartment, hoping that neatness counted when it came to avoiding homicide arrests.

I was just clearing my breakfast dishes from the dining room table when tragedy struck. The knife I'd use to spread strawberry jam on my cinnamon raisin bagels—slick from the butter I'd also slathered on—suddenly slipped from my fingers. I watched in horror as it landed smack dab on my fresh-from-the-cleaners khaki pants. Oh, foo. Now I had a big red blob on my khaki crotch!

Dashing to the kitchen, I immediately started dabbing out the stain with water from the sink.

The good news is the stain came out in no time.

The bad news is that my big red blob was now a big wet blob.

Just as I was about to race to the bedroom to change, there was a knock on my door.

Oh, hell. It had to be Detective Adam's Apple.

I stood frozen in panic, debating whether or not to keep him waiting while I changed pants.

Another knock.

"Ms. Austen?" It was Adam's Apple's voice, all right. "Are you there?"

Dammit. I couldn't leave him standing outside. I just hoped he wouldn't notice a stain the size of Rhode Island on my crotch.

Reluctantly I opened the door.

"Detective Adam's . . . I mean, Detective Willis. Come in, won't you?"

"Thanks," he said, his eyes riveted on the wet spot on my pants.

So much for him not noticing.

"Excuse my pants. I just had a little accident."

"Really? You know, there's medication you can take for that."

"No, I meant an accident in the kitchen. I spilled some jam on my pants. And I was washing the stain out. This is just water!" I hastened to assure him.

At which point, Prozac came sashaying over to join us.

She does stuff like this all the time.

"Look who's here!" he cried, sweeping her up in his arms.

Prozac proceeded to purr like a buzz saw.

I like this one so much better than Old Denture Breath.

"Excuse me," I said, taking advantage of their love-fest, "while I change into something a little drier."

I scooted off to the bedroom to slip on some elastic waist jeans. By the time I got back, Prozac had draped herself across Detective Adam's Apple like a Vegas lap dancer. I almost expected to see a twenty-dollar bill tucked under her collar.

"Why don't you leave the nice man alone?" I said, swooping her off his lap.

She wasted no time shooting me a filthy look.

Party pooper.

"Well," Detective Adam's Apple said, brushing cat hairs from his slacks, "I guess I'd better tell you why I'm here."

I held up a palm to stop him.

"I know why you're here, and I want to tell you you're wrong. I had nothing whatsoever to do with Joy Amoroso's death."

"But, Ms. Austen—"

"And I can't understand why you're focusing on me

when there are so many more viable suspects out there."

And before you could say Benedict Arnold, I was ratting out anyone I could think of. I told him how Joy had been threatening to turn Tonio over to the authorities, and how I was almost certain she had been blackmailing Greg. How Aunt Faith had hated Joy's guts and how Travis had stolen her dating database the minute she was dead. And finally, I told him about Alyce Winters's diabetes syringe and how she could have used it to poison Joy's chocolate.

"Any one of those people could have killed Joy," I said when I'd finally run out of steam. "So why are you here questioning me?"

"Actually I'm not here about the murder."

"You're not?"

Hallelujah! I was a free woman!

"No, I came on a private matter."

"A private matter?"

"Yes. Of a . . . social nature."

Omigosh. He was actually blushing. Was it possible he was interested in me?

Up until that point, I'd viewed Detective Adam's Apple solely as a potential jailer. But now I took a closer look at him. In addition to that prominent Adam's apple of his, he had rather appealing brown eyes and a sweet dimple on his left cheek. And even though his dark hair was cropped close, I could see it was thick and shiny.

All in all, he was a bit of a cutie pie.

Maybe he *was* interested in me. Wouldn't it be something if we started dating and got married and some day we wound up telling our grandchildren the story of how I thought he was coming to arrest me when all along he just wanted to ask me out?

And before I knew it, I was shouting, "Yes!"

"Yes what?" he asked.

Oh, hell. I'd gotten so caught up in my daydream, I'd said yes before he'd even popped the question.

"I meant, 'Yes! I'm so happy you're not here to question me about the murder.' " Then, with an eager smile, I asked, "So what's this private matter you wanted to discuss?"

He cleared his throat, clearly a tad nervous.

Aw, how cute. I felt like patting his hand and telling him he had nothing to worry about, that I just happened to be free for the next 267 Saturday nights.

"Remember how you said you wrote dating profiles for Joy?"

"Yes, I remember," I replied, not exactly thrilled at this conversational turn of events.

"Well, I've just joined one of those Internet dating services, and I was hoping I could hire you to write a profile for me."

So much for our future grandkids.

"I'm really good at writing up criminal cases," he was saying, "but when it comes to personal stuff, I stink."

"I'd be happy to help," I said, most annoyed at myself for having indulged in that absurd daydream.

We agreed on a small fee, and he filled me in on his personal info.

Like me, he was a native Angeleno, born in Manhattan Beach, right next to my home town of Hermosa. When he told me he was into movies, books, and crossword puzzles, I couldn't help but feel excited.

"Me, too!" I cried. "I love movies and books and crossword puzzles. I do the *New York Times* puzzle every day!"

"That's nice," he replied with a mild smile. "I'm also into ultimate Frisbee and beach volleyball."

Cancel that romance. No way was anyone ever going

to get me and my thighs on a beach, playing volleyball. Or ultimate Frisbee, whatever the heck that was.

Now it was time for the Big Question.

"What about looks?"

I don't care what anybody says, in the end, that's all men are really interested in.

"I'm open to all kinds," he said.

"Really?"

"Absolutely!" A pause, and then he added, "Although frankly, if I'm going to be honest, I think I'd prefer a petite blonde."

"Of course you would," I said with a stiff smile.

What did I tell you? Just another shallow jerk in the dating pool.

And you wonder why I never remarried.

"How soon can you write this up?" he asked.

"It won't take me long at all."

He gave me his e-mail address, and I assured him he'd have his dating profile by the next day.

After thanking me for my time and giving Prozac a farewell love scratch, he headed out the door.

I should have been thrilled that I hadn't been arrested.

Instead, I just wanted to throw a Slurpee at the nearest petite blonde.

Chapter 19

When last we saw Greg, those of you who were paying attention and not running to the fridge for a snack will no doubt remember that he'd been heading off to an art gallery with a "freshly painted" oil he'd just hauled out of a dusty closet.

I was pretty much convinced he was a fraud and that somehow Joy had found out about it and was blackmailing him. But I couldn't confront him, not without admitting I'd trespassed on his private property to spy on him.

I needed a way to get him to admit he was faking those paintings of his.

And with a great deal of thought (not to mention a few Double Stuf Oreos), I figured out how to do it.

After a pit stop at my local home supply store, I headed out to Greg's place in Santa Monica.

I was happy to see his Lamborghini in the driveway. Which meant he was home and my plan could proceed unimpeded.

Well, not exactly unimpeded. There were two furry obstacles standing in my way.

Namely, Rocky and Bullwinkle.

What if those rascal rodents were lurking in the front

yard, just waiting for their chance to chomp into my elastic waist jeans?

But if you think a woman of my mental fortitude was about to be intimidated by two pint-sized, pea-brained squirrels—you're absolutely right.

Which is why I'd picked up a can of something called Squirrel-B-Gone at the home supply store.

Clutching it now in my sweaty palm, I scooted up Greg's front path. If Rocky and Bullwinkle came anywhere near me, I intended to let them have it straight in their beady little eyes. But thank heavens all was quiet in Greg's front yard. No sign of my bushy-tailed assailants anywhere.

I made it to the front door without incident and rang the bell, stashing my Squirrel-B-Gone in my purse.

Greg came to the door in his jeans and work shirt, his hands once again immaculately clean.

He frowned at the sight of me.

"You again?" he snapped. "I've said all I have to say about Joy Amoroso."

"But that's not why I'm here," I said, plastering on my brightest smile. "I seem to have lost one of my earrings yesterday, and I'm pretty sure I dropped it in your living room. Mind if I come in for a sec and look around?"

He rolled his eyes, not even trying to hide his annoyance.

"If you must," he sighed, reluctantly letting me in.

Following him into the living room, I made a beeline for the sofa where I'd been sitting yesterday. Immediately I started running my hands between the cushions, eyeing the box of Valentine's candy still on his coffee table.

(Isn't it amazing how some people take *days* to finish a box of chocolates?)

When I figured enough time had elapsed, I cried, "Here it is!"

I then held up an earring I'd been clutching in my hand all along.

"I'm so happy I found it. It's a family heirloom passed down to me from my mom." (It was passed down to me from my mom, all right—via the Home Shopping channel—for $29.68, plus shipping and handling.)

"How touching," Greg said. "Now if you'll excuse me, I've got to get back to my painting."

"Just one more thing," I said, not moving an inch. "I was hoping you could do me a tiny favor. You see, I'm painting my bedroom, and I can't decide which color I like. What with you being an artist, I was hoping you could help me make up my mind."

And before he had a chance to object, I whipped out some paint chips I'd picked up at the home supply store.

"What do you think? Azure? Or Robin's Egg Blue?"

He gave the chips a cursory glance and said, "Robin's Egg Blue."

"That's the blue you prefer?"

"Yes, that's the blue I prefer!" he said with an impatient tap of his work boots.

"Very interesting, I said. "Because both of these paint chips happen to be green."

An angry flush surged up under his tan.

"Get out of here!" he screamed. "Now!"

But I wasn't about to go anywhere.

"You're colorblind, aren't you, Greg? I noticed it yesterday. Your socks didn't match. They still don't."

He looked down at his socks, then up at me.

"So? I'm colorblind. What's the big deal?"

"It's no big deal, not unless you're an artist famed for his use of color."

His eyes darted around the room like he was looking for the nearest emergency exit.

Clearly I had him rattled.

"And if you're so busy painting, how come your hands are so clean? Not a spot of paint anywhere."

"Ever hear of turpentine?" he sneered.

"Sure have. It has quite a distinct smell. Your hands smell like Zest to me."

"Exactly what are you trying to say?"

This was it. The moment I'd been waiting for.

"You're a fraud, Greg. Someone else painted your paintings."

"That's preposterous!"

He tried to look outraged, but it wasn't working. Those darting eyes of his refused to meet mine.

"You can't prove a thing!" he said, a hint of desperation in his voice.

"Oh, yes, I can." I decided to throw caution to the winds and tell the truth. "I happened to be sitting in a tree outside your studio yesterday. I saw you take that dusty old painting out of a closet and tell someone at an art gallery that you'd just finished painting it."

"Okay, that does it!" he said, whipping out his cell phone from his jeans pocket. "I'm calling the cops and having you arrested for trespassing!"

"Great. And while we're waiting for them to show up, I'll call your art gallery and tell them you're a fake."

"It'll be your word against mine." He clamped his arms across his chest in a gesture of defiance. "They'll never believe you."

"I think they will when I tell them about that mysterious closet of yours. Something tells me there may be a whole lot more 'freshly painted' oils stacked up inside."

That was it. Game over. Score one for Jaine.

Shoulders slumped in defeat, Greg clicked his phone shut and sank down into a nearby armchair.

"Joy knew all about this, didn't she?" I asked.

He nodded mutely.

"And she was blackmailing you."

"For five miserable years," he groaned.

"So who really painted your stuff?"

"My uncle George. He died about six years ago. Left me everything in his will. Uncle George painted as a hobby. Never thought of himself as an artist, just kept piling his pictures in the garage. He thought they were worthless, and so did I.

"At first I planned to have them all hauled off to the Goodwill. Except for one painting that I'd hung in my living room. Then one night I brought home a woman I met in a bar. She took one look at the painting and fell in love with it. Saw it was signed G. Stanton and assumed I painted it. I didn't correct her. I was trying to score with her, and I thought that might help. Turns out she worked at an art gallery on Melrose. She brought it in, and the owner put it up on display. Two weeks later it sold for forty-five grand."

He smiled at the memory.

"Needless to say, I canceled that trip to the Goodwill. I realized I had a gold mine on my hands. If I parceled out Uncle George's paintings carefully, I could live on them for the rest of my life.

"Soon I was getting a lot of press, and Uncle George's paintings started selling for more and more money. Everything was going along fine. Until Joy came along."

He slumped even lower in his seat.

"She showed up at one of my gallery exhibits. I knew she was trouble the minute I saw her waddling over to me in one of her tent dresses. She had this smile on her face, like a cat who'd just caught a particularly juicy mouse.

"She said she knew all about my little secret and that unless I joined her crummy dating service and agreed to be photographed with her all over town, she'd tell the world what a fraud I was."

"How on earth did she know about your uncle George?"

"After my Aunt Min died, Uncle George was lonely. He wanted to join Dates of Joy but couldn't afford the initiation fee. So he wrote Joy a letter, asking if she'd accept one of his paintings instead of money. She turned him down flat, of course, money-grubbing bitch that she was.

"Unfortunately Uncle George had enclosed a photo of himself with the painting, and Joy never threw it out. Then, when I made my big splash on the art scene, she saw a picture of me in the paper with one of 'my' paintings. Joy knew I didn't paint it, because she had a picture of Uncle George holding it—date stamped three years before I claimed to have finished it."

Ouch.

"That was all the blackmail ammunition she needed. And so for the past five years I've been paying her a small fortune to keep her mouth shut. I didn't mind the money so much. It was having to constantly show up at her stupid parties, never able to form a relationship because I had to stay single for Joy."

So I'd been right all along about Greg's dubious membership in Dates of Joy.

"Joy claimed she had Uncle George's photo stashed away in a safe deposit box. So I thought I was trapped. Until a few weeks ago when Tonio told me the truth. He and Joy had just had one of their many fights, and he was pissed. He'd always felt sorry for me and confessed that Joy had made up the story about the safe deposit box. She was too cheap to rent one. Uncle George's photo was in a file cabinet in her office.

"I made up my mind to get it. When I bumped into you outside of Joy's office the night of the murder, I was on my way to bust into her file cabinet. Which I did. I found the damn picture. I was free at last."

"So you didn't touch her chocolates?" I asked.

"No, I'm not the one who poisoned her chocolates. But after all Joy put me through, I'm very grateful to whoever did." Then, with a weary sigh, he added: "So how much is it going to cost me to keep you quiet?"

"Nothing."

"Really?" He blinked in disbelief.

"Your uncle left you those paintings. As far as I'm concerned, they're yours to do with as you wish."

And it was true. It was none of my business what Greg Stanton did with his uncle's paintings. All I cared about was whether or not he killed Joy. And at that moment, I have to confess, I believed him when he said he was innocent.

(Then again, I believed The Blob when he promised to cherish me forever, so I'm not exactly infallible.)

"I'm very grateful," Greg said, at last making eye contact with me. "I just hope you won't change your mind."

"I won't change my mind," I assured him. "You don't owe me a thing. Except maybe one of those chocolates over there," I said, nodding to the box of Valentine's chocolates still on his coffee table.

"Of course," he said, hurrying over to get the box. "Here. Keep the whole box."

"Oh, no, one's enough," I said, reaching for a candy.

"You're not really writing a story for the *L.A. Times,* are you?" Greg asked as I bit into a caramel crème.

"No," I confessed with a sheepish smile.

"So what are you up to, anyway?"

"Just poking around, asking questions, trying to find the killer and clear my name. You were right about me being a suspect. The cops think I may have killed Joy."

"If you want to find the real killer," he said, "I suggest you check in with Joy's aunt."

"Aunt Faith?"

"Some old dame who sells wackadoodle jewelry."

"That's Aunt Faith. I met her at Joy's memorial service."

"Tonio tells me that Joy died without a will and that the old lady was her only living relative. Which means she inherits everything. And gives her plenty of reason to want Joy dead, don't you agree?"

I did, indeed.

Chapter 20

I headed for my car with a spring in my step and a box of Valentine's candy under my arm.

(Okay, so I took the whole box.)

It had been quite a productive meeting. I'd confirmed the truth about Greg's paintings and got a lead about Aunt Faith to boot.

It was definitely time to pay Joy's not-so-loving relative a visit.

She'd had nothing but nasty things to say about Joy in her "eulogy," and for all I knew, she'd knocked off her niece to get her hands on a juicy inheritance.

I rummaged around in my purse and fished out the business card she'd given me at the memorial service.

Printed in elegant calligraphy were the words:

FROM TRASH TO TREASURE
RECYCLED JEWELRY FOR THE HIP AT HEART
FAITH COOPERMAN, DESIGNER IN CHIEF

I called the number on the card, and a cheery voice at the other end trilled, "Faith Cooperman here!"

"Hi. I'm Jaine Austen. I don't know if you remember me. We met at Joy's memorial service."

"How could I forget? It's not often I see someone in a CUCKOO FOR COCOA PUFFS T-shirt at a memorial service."

Oops. I'd been hoping no one had noticed it under my blazer.

"Anyhow," I said, plowing past my fashion faux pas, "I was hoping I could stop by and see your jewelry."

Not true, of course. I had no interest whatsoever in her baubles, but it was a good excuse to get some face time with her.

"I just need the address for your shop."

"I don't have a shop, honey. I do most of my sales on eBay. But come on over to my apartment, and I'll be happy to show you what I've got. I just finished a fabulous bracelet made out of lug nuts!"

"Can't wait to see it," I lied.

She gave me her address, and after just two more Valentine's chocolates—okay, four more, but I was skipping lunch, so don't give me any grief—I was on my way to Faith's apartment in the San Fernando Valley community of Tarzana.

Faith lived on a leafy street crammed with low-rise apartment buildings. A lone bungalow stubbornly clung among them, a reminder of what the street had undoubtedly looked like a half a century ago.

I found a parking space outside Faith's building, Tarzana Gardens. As far as I could see, the "gardens" consisted of a row of wilted impatiens bordering a patch of balding grass.

Faith buzzed me in on the building's rusty intercom, and minutes later, she was opening the door to her apartment, clad in an eye-popping floral muumuu and a paper clip necklace. Once again I was struck by her remarkable resemblance to Joy. The same chubby bod, the same thick blond hair, the same turned-up nose and blue eyes.

But then she smiled a broad, welcoming smile, and all similarity to Joy faded away.

Aunt Faith was either a very friendly gal, or she knew how to fake it.

"Come in, come in," she said, ushering me into her living room, a rather shabby avocado and gold affair straight out of a Sears catalog, circa 1972.

"This is my husband, Bert," she said, pointing to a florid sixty-something guy napping on a recliner, an open racing form splayed across his belly.

"Wake up, Bert!" she shouted.

He jolted awake with a snort.

"Say hello to Ms. Austen. She's here to buy my jewelry!"

Oh, hell. I was hoping to window shop on this trip and not actually have to part with any cash.

"Hi there," Bert said, waving a feeble finger.

Faith led me past him to her dining room table, where she had a whole bunch of her Trash to Treasures jewelry spread out. Some of the pieces, I'm afraid, looked like they hadn't quite made it past the trash stage.

"Here's that piece I was telling you about," she said, holding up a heavy hunk of metal. "My lug nut bracelet! Can't you just see yourself in it?"

Only if I was changing a tire.

"And it's just thirty-five dollars!"

Thirty-five dollars for a bunch of lug nuts???

"And how about these?" she gushed. "Zipper earrings!" She held up two miniature zippers dangling from earring posts. "So on trend, aren't they?"

All I could think was that somewhere some leprechaun was missing his fly.

"Or how about this? My toothbrush bracelet!"

Now she was holding up a pink plastic toothbrush

that had somehow been molded into a circle, the bristles painted chartreuse.

"Only forty-five dollars," she said, waving the bristles in my face.

No way was I paying forty-five dollars for a used toothbrush.

I was desperately trying to think of a way out of buying any of this junk when I glanced down at one of the dining room chairs and saw a stack of real estate spec sheets—the kind they hand out at open houses.

"You guys house hunting?" I asked.

"Yes!" Faith beamed. "I got a call from Joy's attorney, and it turns out she died without a will, so I'm her sole beneficiary!" She clapped her hands like a kid who'd just learned she'd won a giant teddy bear at the fair. "What a surprise! I thought for sure she'd have left everything to that greaseball boyfriend of hers. Or her other significant other, her plastic surgeon."

From the recliner, Bert piped up: "That gal had her face lifted so many times, she had nothing left in her shoes."

"I can't decide what to do with the money," Faith was musing. "Buy a new condo in the city, or open my own jewelry store."

"I vote for a condo!" Bert said. "I'm sick of living in the valley."

"It's poetic justice, that's what it is!" Faith rambled on, ignoring the vote from the peanut gallery. "After all Joy put me and her mother through, she owes me. Big time.

"I only hope the police don't think I had anything to do with her death. They were here questioning me the other day. There was no love lost between me and Joy, but I certainly didn't kill her. After all, she was my sister's child."

At last. The conversation was right where I wanted it—on the murder.

"I don't see how the police could possibly suspect you," I said. "I'm sure you were nowhere near Joy's party on Valentine's night. Right?"

If she had an alibi, now was her chance to use it.

"Absolutely not," Faith said. "I've never once stepped foot in that office of hers. Not after the way Joy pulled the rug out from under her mother and me. No, Bert and I were here all night having a romantic Valentine's evening. Weren't we, Bertie?"

Over in his recliner, Bert squirmed, clearly uncomfortable.

"Um . . . right," he said. "We were home all night."

Hmm. Very interesting.

I couldn't tell if he was embarrassed at the memory of the high jinks involved in their "romantic evening." Or if he was uneasy because his wife was lying about being home all night.

"Yes," Faith was saying, "after a lifetime of treachery and abuse, I'm finally getting my just rewards. First thing tomorrow I'm going to put all Joy's designer shoes on eBay and have that Cupid statue in her office appraised. I'm pretty sure it's bronze with gold leaf detail. Should be worth a few grand."

Hold on a sec.

If I wasn't mistaken, I'd just caught Aunt Faith in a bit of a lie.

"But I don't understand," I said. "If you've never set foot in Joy's office, how did you know about the Cupid?"

A merest hint of hesitation before she said, "Oh, I've seen it a million times in those corny ads of hers."

But there was something in that beat of hesitation before she answered, like someone who'd just steadied herself before tripping, that made me wonder if she'd seen that Cupid up close and personal—perhaps on the night of the murder, while she was slipping her niece a poisoned chocolate.

"So what do you think?" she asked, holding up the zipper earrings.

Oh, hell. We were back to the jewelry again. Why did I tell that stupid "I want to buy jewelry" lie in the first place? Why couldn't I have told her my other stupid lie about doing a story for the *L.A. Times?*

"Just twenty-five bucks," she cooed.

I wasn't about to spend twenty-five dollars on a pair of zipper earrings. No way. No how. Never in a zillion years.

I'd simply tell Faith I thought her jewelry was lovely but I'd take a pass. That would be it, clean and simple.

"Do you take personal checks?" were the words that actually came out of my mouth.

What can I say? She was so damn proud of her wacky jewelry, I couldn't say no.

I've actually wound up wearing the earrings a few times. They look sort of cute. Especially with my toothbrush bracelet.

Chapter 21

You know how it is when you think you've finally gotten over a terrible cold and you hop out of bed, ready to rejoin the land of the living, and then you feel that annoying tickle in the back of your throat and let out a whopper of a sneeze and realize the cold you thought had gone away has come back?

Well, that's the way it was with Skip Holmeier. Like a nasty virus, he just wouldn't go away.

When I got home from my visit to Faith that afternoon, the phone was ringing.

I picked it up, blissfully unaware of the virus on the other end.

"Hello, Jaine? It's me. Skip Holmeier III."

Oh, gaak.

"I got your letter," he said, "and I accept the fact that our relationship is over."

Our relationship? What relationship? One bar fight with a blind jazz singer, and lunch at his mother's grave?

"All I ask is that we get together one more time so I can have closure."

"Really, Skip. I don't think that's such a good idea."

Silence on the other end of the line. For a second, I allowed myself to hope that he'd hung up.

No such luck.

"I just came back from my doctor," he finally said with a catch in his voice. "He told me my toe fungus wasn't looking good."

Oh, please. He was playing the toe fungus card! How low could he go?

"In some cases," he whimpered, "it can be fatal."

"I'm sorry, Skip. But my answer is still no."

"If you go out with me, I'll bring pie."

"What day works for you?"

Can you believe it? I pimped myself out for a measly pie!

I was thoroughly disgusted with myself. I should have asked for ice cream, too.

Skip told me he'd pick me up the next morning at ten a.m., and indeed at the crack of ten, there he was on my doorstep, dressed in a nautical blue blazer and white slacks, his toupee peeking out from under a perky sailor's cap.

I had been tempted to dress for the occasion in funereal black (to match my mood) but instead opted for elastic waist pants, I ♥ MY CAT T-shirt, and sweatshirt hoodie.

"How adorable you look!" he cried.

Needless to say, he was not talking to me, but to Prozac.

"Here's your pie." He handed me a large bakery box. "I brought you chocolate cream, just like you requested. Heavy on the whipped cream."

Eagerly accepting my bribe, I trotted off to the kitchen to put it in the fridge. I couldn't wait for this date to end so I could dig into it. Skip had made me promise not to eat the pie in front of him so he wouldn't have to watch me "poisoning" my body.

"I've packed us a delicious picnic basket," he announced when I got back from the kitchen.

I groaned at the thought.

"Are we having lunch at the cemetery again?"

"No, of course not. We're going to Naples."

"Italy??"

No way was I jetting off to Europe with this guy, not without an armed chaperone.

"Naples, California," he corrected me with a hearty chuckle. "It's a charming little cluster of islands just south of Long Beach. We're going to take a gondola ride along the canals."

"Sounds like fun."

And it did. If only I weren't going with Skip.

I grabbed my purse and started for the door when Skip said, "Don't forget Prozac!"

"Prozac?"

"She's coming, too!" he beamed. "I made special arrangements."

"Not a good idea, Skip. Prozac's impossible in a car. I can't even imagine what chaos she'd unleash on a gondola."

Prozac looked up from where she was hard at work shredding my throw pillow to ribbons.

Hey, who are you calling impossible?

Skip turned to me, devastated.

"Please let her come. You'll behave in the car, won't you, Prozac?"

But Prozac was too busy destroying my throw pillow to give him the time of day.

"I've brought caviar for my little princess," he crooned in her ear.

I swear, that cat understands English, because suddenly she forgot about the throw pillow and practically hurled herself into his arms.

Let's get this party started!

Normally the minute you put Prozac in a car, she starts doing the cha-cha around the foot pedals, causing near-fatal accidents. And if she's locked in her carrier, she's been known to wail at the top of her lungs for as long as five and a half straight hours. (If you don't believe me, just ask Virgin Airlines.)

But that day, with the thought of caviar at the end of her rainbow, she was a perfect angel. A regular Emily Post with retractable claws. She trotted into her carrier with nary a whimper, and when I let her out in Skip's Bentley, she sat in my lap, gazing up at Skip with seductive green eyes.

"Love me, snookums?" he crooned.

You bet, Denture Breath. With us it was love at second sight. At first sight, I didn't realize you were loaded.

Naples is normally about a forty-minute drive from L.A. But of course with Skip behind the wheel, it took us close to two agonizing hours.

I figured I might as well take advantage of our alone time to ask a few questions about the murder. Maybe Skip saw something at the party that would lead me to the killer.

"I still can't get over the way Joy was poisoned," I said.

"A terrible tragedy," Skip clucked. "Are you sure Prozac's comfortable? I've got a down pillow in the back seat, if you think she'd like it."

"She's fine. Getting back to Joy . . ." I prompted.

"Such a lovely lady," Skip reminisced. "Always so kind to me. And to Miss Marple—petting her and playing with her and giving her all those goodies to eat."

"I don't suppose you saw anyone sneaking into her office the night of the party?"

"People were coming and going all night, but I wasn't paying attention to anyone. Except you. I thought I saw you dash across the hall to her office."

"I didn't kill Joy," I hastened to assure him.

"Of course not!" he said. "Nobody who owns a cat as wonderful as Prozac could ever be a killer."

Wow. What a glowing character endorsement.

The rest of the trip passed in an uneventful silence broken only by the curses of our fellow motorists, a tad miffed at Skip for going thirty five miles an hour in the fast lane of the freeway.

At last we arrived at the gondola dock.

It was a glorious day, just a few cotton-puff clouds in a turquoise sky.

Skip parked his Bentley and took out his picnic basket from the trunk.

With Prozac safely back in her carrier, we walked along a pier of weathered wooden planks.

"Did you remember to bring an extra sweater?" Skip asked. "It can get a little chilly out on the canals."

"Yes, I've got one right here."

"No, I meant for Prozac."

"I'm sure she'll be fine."

"No matter. I brought an ermine shawl she can use."

A slim athletic fellow in a blue and white striped shirt and straw hat greeted us at the end of the pier with a friendly "Buongiorno!"

From his bright red hair and freckles, I guessed he probably wasn't Italian.

"Welcome to the *Mona Lisa*," he said, gesturing to a sleek black gondola straight out of the canals of Venice. "My name is Kevin, and I'll be your gondolier on your romantic gondola getaway."

Whoa, Nelly! Did I just hear the word "romantic?"

"Just FYI, Kevin," I piped up. "This is going to be a strictly platonic gondola ride. Right, Skip?"

"If you say so, my dear," he said with a most infuriating wink.

Kevin helped us aboard the narrow craft, and we settled down onto a wooden bench seat that had been lined with plump pillows and blankets to lay across our laps.

I made a point of putting my sweater between Skip and me, just in case he got any ideas.

"And who do we have here?" Kevin asked, peering into Prozac's carrier.

"My cat, Prozac."

By now Prozac was meowing at the top of her lungs, eager to get out and join the party.

A twinge of panic clutched my heart as I opened the latch; heaven only knew what Prozac would do once she was let loose on the *Mona Lisa*. I just prayed she wouldn't dive overboard at the sight of a juicy fish swimming by.

Gingerly I took her out.

"Buongiorno, Prozac!" Kevin greeted her.

She eyed his straw hat with interest. For a minute I feared it was a goner. But then, no doubt remembering the caviar to come, she restrained herself and curled up in a ball on my lap.

"Ready to set sail?" asked Kevin.

After we assured him we were ready for our grand adventure, Kevin plopped his oar into the water and began rowing across the bay that separated Naples from the mainland.

Skip wasted no time opening his picnic basket and taking out a jumbo jar of caviar, along with some toast squares, chopped hard-boiled eggs, and a bottle of champagne.

Popping open the champagne bottle, he poured us each a glass.

Then the moment Prozac had been waiting for: Skip opened the caviar. And before you could say Holy Beluga, Prozac jumped into his lap, waiting for the feast to begin.

Lay it on me, big boy.

Her wish was his command.

Taking a tiny spoon from the basket, he started hand-feeding her beluga's finest.

Needless to say, Prozac was in seventh heaven.

I, however, was not a fan of fish eggs, so I had to settle for nibbling on toast squares and hard-boiled eggs. Not too bad, especially when washed down with a snootful of champagne.

After a few sips of the bubbly, I was beginning to feel quite mellow. By now we had reached the islands of Naples. I leaned back against the pillows, snuggled under a blanket, as Kevin steered the gondola along the canals, pointing out the sights. I looked up at the spectacular homes that lined our route, daydreaming of some day living there with proceeds from the sale of my Great American Novel.

Skip had, thank goodness, shown no signs of getting romantic. Not with me, anyway. He was saving all his love for Prozac, stroking her fur with each spoonful of caviar.

After cruising the canals for a while, we reached a bridge spanning two of the islands.

Kevin stopped rowing and glided to a halt under the structure.

"This is Lovers' Bridge," he announced.

Uh-oh. I didn't like the sound of this.

"Tradition has it that lovers are supposed to kiss and seal their love here, under the bridge."

Clearly my little talk about platonic friendship had not sunk in.

"Don't worry," he added with a wink. "I won't look." And with that, he turned his back to us and started belting out a rather ear-piercing version of "O Sole Mio."

Meanwhile Skip was staring at me with moony eyes.

I certainly hoped he didn't expect to cop a kiss from me. If he did, I was prepared to bean him over the head with his own champagne bottle.

But much to my relief, Skip didn't make any move toward me. Instead he reached into his pocket and took out a small turquoise box.

Omigod. I'd recognize that color anywhere. It was Tiffany blue.

"Open it," he said, handing it to me.

For a terrifying instant I thought it might be an engagement ring, but when I lifted the lid, I saw it was a bracelet. I held it up. Even in the shadow of the bridge it was sparking like a zillion candles.

"These aren't diamonds, are they?" I asked.

"Ten carats' worth," he nodded.

Holy Moses! It had to be worth a fortune. It took every ounce of willpower I possessed to say, "The bracelet is gorgeous, but I can't possibly accept it."

"No worries," Skip said. "It's not a bracelet, and it's not for you."

Huh?

"It's a collar, and it's for Prozac."

At the sound of her name, Prozac looked up from where she had been industriously licking the lid of the caviar jar.

For moi?

And before I could stop him, Skip snatched the collar from me and fastened it around Prozac's neck.

She looked up at him with coy green eyes.

Your place or mine?

By now, Kevin had finished mangling "O Sole Mio" and we were back in the sunshine, heading to the dock.

"I'm sorry, Skip," I said, "but Prozac can't accept the collar, either."

I reached out to unfasten it from her neck, but the minute I did, she turned into The Beast With a Thousand Claws.

No way was I getting that collar off her neck without capsizing the gondola.

"I'll take it off when we're home," I promised, "and return it to you then."

Skip held up his hand in protest.

"No! You must keep it. I insist! So how about it, Jaine?" he asked, his cataracts misting over with emotion. "Will you make me the happiest man in the world and give me your hand in marriage?"

"I'm sorry, Skip, but I can't."

"Okay, then will you make me the happiest man in the world and give me your cat?"

"No, I won't give you Prozac!"

"I'll pay you twenty-five grand."

"Twenty-five grand?" I gasped.

Prozac perked up, interested.

I'm worth every penny.

I sat there in stunned disbelief, aghast at the idea of selling my beloved kitty.

I thought back to the day I first saw her at the shelter, a scrawny critter snoring in the corner of her cage. I remembered how I picked her up and felt her tiny heart thumping wildly against my chest. And how, when I brought her back to my apartment, she curled up in a ball on my sofa and looked up at me, gratitude beaming from her big green eyes, as if to say, *I'm home at last.*

Okay, so maybe she didn't exactly curl up on my sofa. Maybe she ran around my apartment, attacking my plants, chewing on my electrical cords and clawing my coffee table, looking up at me as if to say, *So when do we eat?*

But still, the little furball had wormed her way into my heart, and I wasn't about to let her go.

"Forget it," I told Skip.

"I'll throw in another pie," he said, a hopeful look in his eyes.

Resisting the impulse to ask what kind, I shook my head, my answer still an unequivocal no.

We drove home in silence, Skip staring mournfully ahead.

I made a few stabs at small talk, but he wasn't having any.

When we finally turned up the street to my duplex, I put Prozac back in her carrier. "I'll get that collar back to you as soon as I can."

A yelp of protest from the carrier.

Like hell she will!

"And thanks for the pie."

"About that pie . . ." Skip hesitated a sheepish beat. "It's not exactly chocolate cream."

"What is it? Banana cream? Apple? Cherry?"

"Soy-carob, with a wheat germ crust."

"You've got to be kidding!"

"Some day you'll thank me, Jaine," he said with the self-righteous nod of a health food fanatic.

"And what day would that be?" I muttered. "When hell freezes over?"

Swallowing my irritation, I flounced out of the Bentley and headed up the path to my apartment.

Was he the most infuriating man ever, or what?

Of course, that was just one gal's opinion.

From her carrier, I could hear Prozac meowing.

Call me soon, big boy!

Chapter 22

Skip's soy-carob pie was inedible, of course. (Think Elmer's Glue in a wheat germ crust.)

After just one bite, it went sailing into the trash.

Even Prozac, who has been known to nosh on old gym socks, would not go near it.

Of course, after her caviar binge, Prozac was turning her nose up at anything and everything I put in her bowl. It would take weeks of hissing, scratching and yowling at the moon (by me) to get her to eat cat food again. But that's a whole other story, one I'm saving for a licensed psychotherapist.

In the meanwhile, I had to get that damn collar off her neck.

I tried several times to undo the clasp while she was napping, but all I had to show for it was an arm criss-crossed with cat scratches.

I tried diverting her with Hearty Halibut Guts, always a sure fire distraction in the BC (Before Caviar) days.

But she just sniffed at her bowl in disdain.

What—no Beluga?

Well, if she thought I was going to run out and buy ridiculously expensive caviar, she was crazy.

I stuck to my guns and bought ridiculously expensive shrimp instead.

After cutting the shrimp into tidbits (scarfing down a few morsels for myself), I set them down before her with bated breath.

Would she fall for it? Would she dive right in and not look up till every morsel had disappeared down her gullet?

I'm happy to report the answer was yes!

Before I knew it, she had her little pink nose buried in the bowl, oblivious to everything around her.

Wasting no time, I reached over and sprang open the clasp on that damn collar.

At last I held the sparkly diamonds in my sweaty hands.

For a minute, I was tempted to try it on as a bracelet. But I quickly came to my senses and realized I hadn't a second to spare. I had to hide the damn thing before she inhaled the last of her shrimp and came up for air.

I raced to my bedroom where I tucked the collar back in its Tiffany box. I'd just finished shoving it into the far reaches of the top shelf of my closet when there was a knock on my front door.

I hurried to the living room to get it.

By now Prozac had finished her snack and was scratching her neck in outraged disbelief.

Hey! I've been robbed!

Ignoring her indignant yowls, I answered the door.

It was Lance, who came sailing in, waving a copy of the *Beverly Hills Social Pictorial.*

"You'll never guess whose picture is in this week's *Social Pictorial!*"

"Desmond Tutu? Søren Kierkegaard? Jean-Paul Sartre?"

"No, silly. Mine!"

He held up the magazine, and indeed, there was Lance grinning into the camera with a handsome hottie I could only assume was his new squeeze, Donny Johnson.

"Donny and I were at the opening of an amazing new men's boutique on Rodeo Drive when a photographer came up and took our picture." He gazed down at the photo with a sigh. "Isn't Donny gorgeous?"

"I guess, if you're into tall guys with hot bods, great hair, and James Dean cheekbones."

"And look what he bought me," he said, whipping a wallet out of his pocket.

"Oh, dear. Something tells me some poor alligator has given up his life to hold your singles."

"Isn't Donny the most generous guy ever?" he gushed.

I had to admit the guy was awfully loose with a buck.

"And doesn't he have the sexiest smile? Just look at those teeth. Aren't they fabulous?"

I was not, however, looking at Donny's teeth. Something else in the *Social Pictorial* had caught my eye: A photo spread of Beverly Hills partygoers. There among them was Greg Stanton, arm in arm with the stunning brunet I'd seen him with at Simon's. The caption under the picture read, *Famed artist Gregory Stanton with fiancée Lady Penelope Ashford, daughter of British billionaire philanthropist, Sir Wallace Ashford.*

"I don't believe it!" I cried.

"I didn't, either. I thought for sure his teeth were veneers. But they're real! I asked."

"Listen, Lance," I said, wrenching the topic away from Donny's teeth, "do you mind if I keep this *Social Pictorial?*"

"Not at all, hon. I just happened to pick up copies for seventy-five of my nearest and dearest friends."

"Thanks," I said, grabbing it from him eagerly.

"Hey, what's with Prozac?" he said, nodding at my pouting princess, who had been whining nonstop ever since he walked in the door.

"Oh, she's just ticked off because I took away her diamond collar."

Prozac looked up at Lance imploringly.

Quick! Call the police! I'm prepared to press charges!

"Diamond collar?" Lance asked, eyes popping.

"You're not the only one with a generous suitor."

"Omigod. Are you still dating the rich old coot Joy fixed you up with? I knew all along it would work out. We're going to have our double wedding, after all!"

"God forbid," I moaned.

"I want to hear every detail of your romance, hon," he said, oblivious to my glaring lack of enthusiasm. "But not right now. I've got to dash and hand out copies of the *Social Pictorial.*"

And with that, he was off to share his new-found fame with seventy-four of his nearest and dearest.

The minute Lance left, I settled down on the sofa with the *Social Pictorial,* staring at the photo of Greg and his fiancée.

So that brunet he'd been playing kneesies with at Simon's was a British royal. A filthy rich royal, at that. He sure had won the matrimonial sweepstakes, hadn't he? And without Joy in his life, he was free to tie the knot.

As innocent as he'd seemed when last we spoke, I couldn't help thinking that maybe he'd slipped Joy a poisoned chocolate so he could hustle down the aisle with British royalty.

I was sitting there, counting the face-lifts in the *Social Pictorial* and wondering if Lady Penelope Ashford was engaged to a murderer, when the phone rang.

I answered it warily, afraid it might be Skip.

But, much to my relief, a woman's voice came on the line.

"Jaine, this is Alyce Winters, the woman you interviewed for the *L.A. Times.*"

Of course. The Press-On Nail Queen. With the handy dandy diabetes syringe.

"I called to apologize. I'm afraid I was a wee bit intoxicated when you came to see me. I'm so sorry I had you root around in my carpet for my press-on nail."

"Oh, I didn't mind," I lied.

"I'm so ashamed of my behavior. I just called to make sure you don't mention me by name in your article. I'd never be able to live it down."

I assured her that her penchant for brandy at ten in the morning was safe with me, and was about to hang up when she said: "Just one more thing, Jaine. You asked me the other day if I remembered seeing anyone go into Joy's office the night of the murder. At the time, I didn't remember anything—mainly because I was three sheets to the wind. But I've thought about it, and now I do remember seeing someone."

"You do?"

I sat up with a jolt. Was Alyce about to give me an actual lead?

"Yes. It was a young man, an awkward looking fellow, with one of those pocket protectors on his shirt."

Chapter 23

Whaddaya know? It looked like Barry, aka Mr. Pocket Protector, had been at Joy's Valentine's party. Which meant I had a brand new suspect on my list.

Wasting no time, I put in a call to Travis and got Barry's contact info. When I called him there was no answer, so I left a message on his voice mail, urging him to get back to me ASAP.

By now Prozac had leaped to the top shelf of my bookcase next to her favorite author, P. G. Wodehouse, clearly furious at me for nabbing her diamond collar.

"Prozac, honey, won't you please come down!" I begged. "I'll scratch your back for as long as you like."

But she just glared down at me with slitted eyes.

I want a divorce.

I was in the middle of trying to lure her down with some human tuna when the phone rang.

"Jaine? It's Barry Potter, returning your call."

As if the poor guy didn't have enough troubles, he had to be saddled with a name like Barry Potter.

"I don't know if you remember me, Barry. I was there the day you signed up with Dates of Joy."

"I remember you. You tried to warn me about Joy. I should have listened. She turned out to be a very evil lady. Anyhow, I'm sorry I didn't pick up when you called, but we've been busy taking inventory here at Shoe City. That's where I work, you know. We have some great deals on extra-wide orthotic insoles, if you're interested."

"Sounds mighty tempting, Barry, but actually I was hoping you could answer a few questions about Joy Amoroso's murder."

"Sorry, no can do. Phil said I'm not allowed to talk about the murder."

"Phil?"

"My brother-in-law. He's an attorney. Well, technically he's a paralegal, but he knows practically as much as an attorney, and he told me to keep my mouth shut."

Uh-oh. Time to haul out my *L.A. Times* ruse.

"But this isn't really about the murder. I'm writing an exposé for the *L.A. Times* about Joy and her unscrupulous business practices."

"You write for the *L.A. Times?*" he asked, clearly impressed. "That's super!"

"Anyhow, I was hoping you'd be willing to talk about your experiences with Joy. Anonymously, of course," I hastened to assure him. "Your privacy would be totally protected."

"And I'd get to tell the world what a lying, cheating witch of a woman she was?"

"Absolutely."

"Then count me in!"

We agreed to meet at his Glendale apartment the next night and I hung up, wondering why on earth he felt the need to arm himself with an attorney.

Barry greeted me at the door of his modest one-bedroom apartment in slacks and a short-sleeved sport shirt, his pocket protector chock full of pens.

"Come on in," he said, waving me into his spartan living room, which consisted of a sofa, coffee table, plastic lawn chair, and an old fashioned TV hulking in the corner.

In the center of the coffee table, next to a copy of *Shoe Biz* magazine, was a large goldfish bowl.

"Don't worry, Penelope," he called out to the goldfish swimming frantically inside. "It's only Ms. Austen. She's here to interview me for the *Los Angeles Times*."

Then he turned to me and whispered, "She gets anxious around strangers. Don't pay any attention to her and she'll calm down."

A shoe salesman with a neurotic goldfish. No wonder the poor guy had trouble lining up dates.

I sat on the lawn chair, as far from the lap-swimming Penelope as I could get.

"Where's your recorder?" Barry asked, plopping down on the sofa. "Don't all reporters tape their interviews?"

"Oh, no. That's only on TV and in the movies. I've got a fabulous memory!"

"Wow." He gazed at me, awestruck. "That's wonderful. I have a hard time at Shoe City remembering which shoes go in the right box."

"So," I said with a bright smile. "Ready to get started on the exposé?"

I was hoping once I got him warmed up, I could somehow segue into the murder.

"Am I ever!" he said.

And he was off to the races.

"Joy Amoroso was a liar and a cheat. The minute I signed over my CD to her, she wanted nothing to do with me. Put that in the paper," he directed me. "She took people's money and then forgot they were even alive. One day I called her to ask why she hadn't set me up with Albany the model. She thought she put me on hold, but I heard her yelling at her assistant for putting me through to her, and saying that nobody as pretty as Albany would ever go out with a loser like me. "She called me a loser," he said, an angry flush spreading across his face.

"It's not like I didn't already know it, but hearing it out loud was like a sock in my gut. It was then I realized Joy was never going to fix me up with my dream date. Or any date. She took my life savings. Every penny I had. For nothing. "I was so damn mad, I felt like killing her.""

I looked down and saw his fists clenched tight in his lap.

"I didn't, of course," he hastened to add.

"So what happened when you went to the Valentine's party?" I asked, waiting to see if he'd admit he'd been there. "Did you meet anyone?"

He shook his head.

"I took one look at all the middle-aged ladies inside, and I turned around and went home."

So Alyce was right. He had been at the party.

But had he really taken one look at the partygoers and left?

Time for another fib.

"That's funny," I said. "I could've sworn I saw you heading into Joy's office."

"So what if I did?" he said, beads of sweat popping up on his brow. "That doesn't mean I did anything wrong."

"No, of course not. But do you mind my asking what you were doing there?"

He squirmed uncomfortably, his face flushed a deep crimson. For a minute, I thought he was going to get up and make a run for it, but then he slumped down on the sofa and groaned: "Okay, okay. I did it."

Holy mackerel. Had Barry Potter just confessed to Joy's murder?

"You poisoned Joy's chocolate?"

"No, of course not! I stole Albany's headshot."

So much for a murder confession.

"I took Joy's date book from the reception area and brought it into her office. At first I just wanted to look at Albany's picture. I don't know what came over me, but then I took the picture out of the book. I figured Joy owed me that much. I even had it framed."

With that, he reached under the sofa cushion and pulled out a framed photo of the gorgeous redhead he'd fallen for on his first visit to Joy.

"But I'm afraid to hang it up. After all, it's stolen property."

"I wouldn't worry about it if I were you, Barry."

"You're not going to tell?"

"My lips are sealed," I said, getting up to leave.

"No!" he shouted, jumping up and blocking my path. "You can't leave."

All traces of the scared rabbit he'd been just a few seconds ago were gone, his fists once again clenched tight, a strange manic gleam in his eyes.

And a wave of fear shot through me.

Was it possible this namby-pamby goldfish lover was a killer? Had he poisoned Joy's chocolate, after all, and taken Albany's headshot as a souvenir?

Had he known all along I wasn't really a reporter? Had he heard that I was investigating Joy's murder? Afraid I'd stumble onto the truth, had he lured me here to the wilds of Glendale to put a permanent end to me and my investigation?

Suddenly those upper arms of his which just two seconds ago had seemed sort of flabby now looked taut and muscular.

"I've got something to show you," he said.

I just prayed it wasn't a machete.

I surreptitiously reached into my purse for my travel-sized can of Aqua Net. I've always found hair spray an effective substitute for Mace. All it takes is one good spritz in the eye to put your attacker out of commission.

With my finger on the nozzle, I watched as Barry pulled out a drawer in the coffee table and took out a black oblong box.

The perfect size for a revolver.

By now my palms were gushing sweat.

He lifted the lid on the box, and I practically swooned with relief. Not a gun in sight. Instead the box was lined with pens!

"My vintage fountain pen collection," he said, beaming with pride.

Before my grateful eyes, his upper arms turn to flab again.

How foolish I'd been to think of him as a killer.

"I have one of the best collections in the San Fernando Valley. I thought you might be interested in doing a story about them for the *L.A. Times*."

The poor guy just collected pens as a hobby.

"Look," he was saying. "Here's a 1920 Esterbrook. Extra-fine nib."

He took out one of the pens, a lovely tortoiseshell affair, and unscrewed the top. The nip was indeed fine as a needle.

He then unscrewed the base of the pen, revealing the rubber sack that held the ink.

"It's a real beauty isn't it?"

"Absolutely," I said. I wanted to kiss the darn thing, so grateful that it wasn't a lethal weapon.

And then it hit me. Maybe it *was* a lethal weapon. How easy it would have been for Barry to take one of his pens and fill it with cyanide, and use a superfine nib to inject the poison in a bonbon.

Was I looking at an innocent pen—or a murder weapon?

"So how about it, Jaine?" Barry was asking. "Do you think you can write about my pens?"

"I'll have to check with my editor," I fumphered, surreptitiously clutching my Aqua Net. "In the meanwhile, I'd better be running along."

"I hope you got everything you came for," Barry said.

"And then some," I assured him.

YOU'VE GOT MAIL!

TAMPA VISTAS TATTLER

Tampa Vistas residents were treated to a fascinating slide show last night at the town house of Homeowners Association president Lydia Pinkus, whose brother, Professor Lester Pinkus, entertained one and all with a PowerPoint presentation of his recent trip to Nepal, where Mr. Pinkus, along with his colorful Sherpa guide, climbed the rugged cliffs of Mount Gauri Sankar.

The slide show came to an unfortunate halt, however, when one of the partygoers, Mr. Hank Austen, shattered a plate glass window in Mr. Pinkus's bedroom.

Further details were unavailable at press time.

To: Jausten
From: Shoptillyoudrop
Subject: I Thought I'd Die

I thought for sure Daddy had given up on the idea that Lydia and Lester had stolen my ring. He certainly was all smiles when we showed up for the party, running to the buffet and scarfing down Edna Lindstrom's Swedish meatballs like he hadn't just finished a three-course meat loaf dinner at home!

Then the lights dimmed, and we all gathered around to watch Lester's slide show. We weren't sitting there for

more than two minutes, watching Lester and his colorful
Sherpa guide trekking up Mt. Ravi Shankar, when suddenly
I realized Daddy was gone. At first I thought he'd made a
trip to the bathroom, but when five more minutes passed
and he didn't come back, I knew something was up.

As much as I hated to miss the pictures of Lester and his
colorful native guide pitching their tent in their long johns, I
slipped out of the living room to find Daddy. I tried Lydia's
bedroom, the den, and the kitchen (always a popular stop
for Daddy). Finally I came to the guest bedroom.

When I opened the door, I thought I'd die.

There was Daddy, wearing boxing gloves and a pair of
Lester's Everlast boxing shorts! No doubt a memento from
his amateur boxing days.

"Look, Claudia!" he cried. "A punching bag!"

Indeed, there in the corner of the guest bedroom, Lester
had set up a boxer's punching bag.

"And genuine boxing shorts!" Daddy pointed with pride at
his pilfered shorts. "I always wanted to wear a pair of
these. And try my hand at a punching bag. You know.
Float like a butterfly, sting like a bee!"

He danced around, punching the air, his knees sticking
out like doorknobs, Muhammad Ali on Metamucil.

"The screws on the punching bag need a little tightening,
but my handy dandy Belgian Army Knife will take care of
that." Taking off his boxing gloves, he grabbed his Belgian
Army Knife and began tinkering with the screws attaching
the punching bag to the pole.

"Hank Austen!" I hissed. "Leave that punching bag alone!"

"Don't be silly, Claudia. I know what I'm doing."

Ignoring me like he always does, he kept fiddling with the screws. Then he put on the gloves and started punching the bag. He missed the bag on the first two punches. With the third punch—I still shudder at the memory—he made contact.

Before my horrified eyes, the punching bag came loose from the pole and went sailing across the room and crashing through Lester's window, making the most awful racket and sending shards of glass everywhere!

Within seconds, all the party guests had rushed over to see what had happened.

"Good heavens, Hank!" Lydia cried. "What have you done?"

By now I was burning with shame, but Daddy just stood there in Lester's Everlast shorts, not looking the least bit embarrassed.

"I think your punching bag is broken," he had the nerve to say to Lester.

"You're the one who broke it, Hank!" I cried. "You and your silly Belgian Army Knife. I think you owe the Pinkuses an apology."

Your father looked at me as if I'd just asked him to go skinny-dipping in a sewer.

"Me? Apologize to them? Why, they're the ones who owe us an apology."

"Why on earth do we owe you an apology?" Lydia asked.

"For stealing my wife's diamond ring!" Daddy cried, stomping over to Lester's night table.

And then, to my utter amazement, he opened the drawer and took out my Valentine's ring!

"See?" he said to me. "I told you Lydia took it. And Lester's been hiding it for her. I found it right before you came in. I'm just happy I got here before they passed it off to their fence."

"My good fellow," Lester said, putting his arm around Daddy's shoulder, "I'm afraid you've got this all wrong. I didn't steal your wife's ring. I bought this ring from a man in the parking lot at Costco."

"And just when were you planning on wearing it?" Daddy asked, oozing skepticism. "On your next trip to Nepal?"

"I bought it for a lady friend."

"What lady friend?" Daddy asked, Mr. District Attorney.

"Edna Lindstrom," Lester replied, blushing.

"Me?" Edna squeaked.

"I know it's rushing things a bit since we haven't even gone out yet," Lester said, "but those pink stones made me think of your pink cheeks. Speaking of which, did you ever get my Valentine's gift? Two dozen pink roses? I signed the card 'From Your Secret Admirer' and left them at your front door."

"So that's who those flowers were for!" I said. "You left them on our doorstep by mistake, and Hank thought you had a crush on me."

"So you see," Lester said to Daddy, "it's all a big misunderstanding. Let's agree to let bygones be bygones, shall we?"

"We'll pay for a new window, of course," I assured him.

"We'll do no such thing!" Daddy sputtered. "You're not really falling for his story about buying a diamond ring for a woman he's never even gone out with? Puh-leese. What a bunch of dog doo. This is your ring, Claudia, the one Lydia stole from you at Le Chateaubriand, and we're not forking over a dime for that window. Not unless The Evil Axis wants us to press charges for grand theft!"

And with that, he grabbed me and the ring and marched me out of Lydia's town house. It wasn't until we got home that I realized Daddy was still wearing Lester's Everlast shorts.

Oh, dear. I'm afraid Lydia may never speak to me again.

Your heartsick,
Mom

To: Jausten
From: DaddyO
Subject: Victory!

Well, Lambchop, I'm happy to report that, after a
practically flawless reconnaissance expedition, I've
retrieved your mom's stolen ring from The Evil Axls. I knew
all along that Devious Duo were up to no good.

Love 'n' cuddles from
Your crime-fighting,
Daddy

Chapter 24

I almost choked on a cinnamon raisin bagel the next morning when I read about Daddy's mortifying encounter with Lester Pinkus's punching bag. It's at times like this that I'm very grateful for the three thousand miles separating L.A. and Tampa Vistas.

My heart went out to Mom, but I simply couldn't spend time worrying about the Great Punching Bag Fiasco. Not while I still had that pesky murder to solve.

I had scads of suspects but not a shred of evidence linking any of them to the crime.

Then I flashed on Cassie, Joy's beleaguered personal assistant. It was hard to picture her as a killer, but maybe she'd seen something the night of the murder that would help me solve the crime.

I found her number on Travis's contact list and rang her up.

"Hi, Jaine," she said when she came on the line. "I've been expecting your call."

"You have?"

"Travis told me you've been snooping around, asking questions about the murder."

"Guilty as charged. I was hoping you and I could have a little talk."

"Honestly, Jaine, I don't think I'm going to be much help."

"Can I stop by to see you anyway? It won't take long. I promise."

Who knew? Maybe with a little prompting, I could get her to remember a vital clue.

"Well, okay," she said, "but you're wasting your time."

She agreed to meet me at her bungalow in Venice later that afternoon.

I was just heading to the bathroom for a quick shower when there was a knock on my door.

I opened it to find Detective Adam's Apple.

Oh, groan. I'd e-mailed him his dating profile days ago. What did he want me to write now? His grocery list?

"Oh, hi," I said with a faint smile. "Can I help you?"

"Yes, you can," he replied rather sternly. "You can stop pretending to be a reporter for the *L.A. Times*."

Oopsie.

"Apparently you've been running around telling people you're writing an exposé on Joy Amoroso."

"Just trying to get information to clear my name. When last I checked, I was one of your suspects."

"Leave the detecting to the professionals, okay? I may be clueless about dating, but I'm fairly competent at tracking down killers."

"Just as long as you don't wind up arresting me. Ha ha."

I waited for a laugh. Or a smile. A flash of that dimple in his left cheek. But he remained stony-faced. Which did not boost my confidence. Not one iota.

"So how's the search coming along for Ms. Right?" I asked in a desperate attempt to change the subject.

"Actually I met a woman I really like."

So he found his petite blonde.

Life isn't fair, is it? Women wait for years to meet their Prince Charming. Or even a decent frog. And men go online and get hooked up practically minutes after they click the SEARCH button.

"We've chatted a few times," he was saying. "And she's got some special qualities that really appeal to me."

Whaddaya bet they both fit into a 34C?

"I want to ask her out, but I don't have the nerve to do it on the phone, so I wrote her a note."

He took a small piece of paper from his pocket.

"I was wondering if you'd mind looking it over just to make sure it's okay," he said, handing it to me.

His missive was short and to the point:

Hi, there!
I've really enjoyed chatting with you. I think
you're cute and funny. Would you like to go out
with me Saturday night?

He was no Shakespeare, but the note was sweet in its simplicity.

"So what do you think?" he asked.

"I think it's just fine."

"Really?"

"Really."

"Thanks so much, "he grinned, his dimple at last making an appearance. "Wish me luck."

I wished him luck, and as I watched him walk away, I secretly hoped his petite blonde showed up for their date with a zit on her nose.

Cassie lived in a dollhouse of a bungalow several blocks from the ocean in Venice.

I made my way past her white picket fence, choked

with roses and geranium vines, up the short path to her bright red front door. Forest-green shutters bracketed the two windows on either side of the entrance, and a squat chimney jutted out from a deeply slanted roof.

It was like a kid's drawing of a house come to life.

How funny to think of goth Cassie with her tattoos and nose ring living in this storybook cottage.

She came to the door in black sweats and oversized T-shirt, her purple hair gelled into fearsome spikes. A tattoo of the words *Ultio Dulcis Est* was visible on her shoulder. What the heck was that? A new rock group? A family motto? A Kama Sutra position?

"C'mon in," she said, leading me into a tiny living room furnished in a wild combo of white wicker and black velvet. Her walls had been painted a deep purple (to match her hair?) and on her scrubbed pine coffee table, next to a vase of peonies, was a human skull filled with Tootsie Rolls.

It was all very Laura Ashley meets Sid Vicious.

"What a charming place," I said. "It's so . . . eclectic."

"Schizophrenic is more like it, but it works for me."

At which point a piercing scream filled the air. For a frightening instant I thought it was the skull on her coffee table come to life. But it was only her teakettle.

"I was just making myself a cup of tea," Cassie said. "Want some?"

"No, thanks," I replied, surprised she wasn't brewing eye of newt. "I'm fine."

As she headed off to her kitchen, I wandered over to look at some photos on her tiny fireplace mantel.

I blinked in disbelief at a picture of a wide-eyed little girl in a pink pinafore with matching pink shoes, a bow in her blond ringlets. In spite of all the changes the years had brought, I recognized that little face. It was pre-tattoo

Cassie. Who would've thought the goth goddess had once worn pink Mary Janes?

"Can you believe what a dorky kid I was?" she said, joining me at the mantel, a mug of tea in her hands.

"You were adorable. You still are."

"My mom was the pretty one in my family."

She handed me a framed photo of a stunning young woman, pale and blond, smiling into the camera with a far-off look in her eyes.

Something about her looked familiar.

"What a beautiful woman," I said, gazing down at the picture. "Was she in the movies?"

"No," she laughed, "not at all. She worked in the perfume department at Saks."

"I bet she's still a beauty."

"Not really." Her eyes clouded over. "She's dead."

"I'm so sorry."

"Me, too."

She curled up in an armchair, cradling her mug of tea in her hands.

"Grab a seat," she said, forcing a smile.

I plunked myself down on the wicker sofa.

"Tootsie Roll?" she offered, gesturing to the skull on the coffee table.

For one of the few times in my life, I said no to chocolate.

"It's lucky you called today," Cassie said. "You caught me on my day off."

"You got another job?"

"I'm cutting hair at Benjamin's, a beauty salon in Brentwood."

"That's terrific."

"It's what I trained to do. I've got my cosmetology degree and everything."

"Then why were you working for Joy?"

"When I first started out in the salon biz, it seemed too cutthroat. So I took a job at Dates of Joy. Of course," she added with a bitter laugh, "I didn't know the true meaning of 'cutthroat' until I started working for Joy."

"I don't suppose you have any idea who might have killed her?"

"As a matter of fact," she said, taking a sip of her tea, "I do."

Holy Moses. It looked like I'd struck gold.

"Who is it?"

"Not telling," she said, with an emphatic shake of her purple spikes.

"Why on earth not?"

"Because whoever killed Joy did the world a favor. She was a vicious bitch and didn't deserve to live."

She spat that last bit out with such loathing, I suddenly wondered if the "killer" she was talking about was Cassie herself.

I remembered those dahlias she'd brought to Joy's memorial service, the ones she knew Joy would have detested. Had Cassie finally snapped under the pressure of working for Joy and killed her boss from hell?

But that didn't make sense. If everybody ran around killing their difficult bosses, half of corporate America would be dead by sunset. Sure, Joy was a bitch on wheels, screaming at Cassie for bringing her Sweet'n Low instead of Splenda, but that didn't seem like motive enough for murder.

"Really, Cassie. If you know who killed Joy, you owe it to the police to speak up."

"The only thing I owe anybody is a decent haircut. Speaking of which, how'd you like me to trim your bangs? They're getting a little ragged."

And just like that she was back to her old self, smiling the same innocent smile she'd beamed in her pink pinafore.

Cassie may have hated Joy, but I simply couldn't see her as a killer.

I begged her to tell me who the culprit was, but she refused to part with her secret.

I left her bungalow as confused as when I'd shown up, not a millimeter closer to the truth.

But on the plus side, my bangs looked great.

Chapter 25

Back home, Prozac was still in a Pout Royale over her diamond collar, holed up with P. G. Wodehouse, coming down only for her meals and then hurling herself back up the bookcase, as far away from me as she could get.

"I miss you, Pro, honey!" I called up to her after supper that night.

(To prove my love, I'd given her all the anchovies on my pepperoni pizza.)

"Will you come down if I give you a nice long belly rub with extra scratching on your neck?"

She glared at me through narrowed eyes.

Not unless there's a diamond collar on it.

It was beginning to look like she'd never forgive me for taking away that dratted collar. Somehow I had to melt her deep freeze. Maybe a new collar would do the trick, something loaded with bling. I checked my watch. Eight o'clock. I still had time to dash over to my local pet shop before they closed.

Minutes later I was on my way to Pet Palace ("Where Your Pets Always Get the Royal Treatment"). As I drove along, my thoughts drifted back to my meeting with Cassie. How aggravating to think that she actually knew who the murderer was, but wasn't talking.

What a strange girl she was—living in that gothic dollhouse with purple walls and a skull for a candy dish. And *Ultio Dulcis Est,* whatever the heck that meant, tattooed on her shoulder.

And what about that photo of her mother, the ethereal beauty? I couldn't shake the feeling that I'd seen her somewhere before.

By now I'd reached Pet Palace and drove down the steep slope into their underground parking lot. It was fairly deserted at that time of night. Just two other cars and a lot of empty shopping carts. I got out of my Corolla and scooted over to the elevator. Although I saw no one, I had the uneasy sensation I was not alone.

I told myself I was being foolish, that Joy's murder had made me a tad paranoid. Nevertheless I was grateful when the elevator finally showed up. I practically leaped inside, pressing the CLOSE DOOR button, holding my breath until the door finally slid shut.

I rode up the single flight to the main floor, still on edge. But once inside Pet Palace, my heebie jeebies vanished. The place was brightly lit, with lots of colorful displays of adorable dogs and cats. I headed for the collar aisle, and right away I saw what I wanted: a hot pink number studded with rhinestones.

Very Vegas Showgirl.

I just prayed Prozac wouldn't be able to tell the difference between Tiffany and a Kitty Katz Kollar.

Pleased with my purchase, I headed for the cashier to pay for it.

There was no line at the checkout counter, and the clerk on duty, a matronly gal whose name tag read MURIEL, seemed happy to take a break from reading *Soap Opera Digest* to ring up my sale.

"I just love this collar," she said, eyeing my Kitty Katz

special. "I got one for my cat Bubbles, and she just adores it!"

That was encouraging news. If Bubbles—surely a kitty of discriminating tastes—loved it, chances were Prozac would, too.

I headed down to the garage a lot chirpier than I'd been on my ride up.

Stepping out from the elevator, I noticed that all the empty carts were gone. One of the employees must have rounded them up and brought them back upstairs.

I got in my Corolla, hoping Prozac would be curled up under my neck that night, her Kitty Katz rhinestones scratching my chin. Then I started up the steep slope to the street, picturing our purr-filled reunion, when suddenly from out of nowhere a shadowy figure appeared at the top of the driveway, in sweats and a hoodie, pushing a stack of the store's shopping carts.

At first I thought it was a store employee. But then, much to my horror, I saw the shadowy figure give the long line of carts a shove—aiming them straight at my Corolla! Frantically I swerved, trying to avoid the coming onslaught, but I wasn't quite fast enough. The heavy metal carts came smashing into my rear fender with a sickening thud, then careened the rest of the way down the driveway, crashing to a halt at a pole in the garage.

With trembling hands I steered my Corolla back up to the street. Luckily it was still running. I looked around, but the street was empty. My hooded assailant was long gone.

By now a few of the store employees, having heard the crash, came running to my car.

I recognized Muriel, my matronly checkout clerk.

"Are you okay?" she asked, her brow furrowed in concern.

"I'm fine." Aside from the small matter of my heart almost bursting through my chest.

"Great!" she said. "Then you can sign this release form."

I now realized she was carrying a clipboard, which she thrust through my car window.

"Pet Palace is not responsible for any accidents in the parking lot," she informed me. "It says so on all the signs in the garage."

What a touching tableau, n'est-ce pas? Clearly the royal treatment at Pet Palace was not extended to humans.

I signed the release form and pulled out into the street.

"I hope your kitty likes her collar!" Muriel called out to me as I drove off.

Oh, well. At least she had some shred of empathy.

"Because it's not returnable!" she added with a jaunty wave.

I was sure that whoever hurled those carts at me was the killer, trying to put the fear of God in me.

And it worked.

I drove home, blood pressure soaring, knuckles white on the steering wheel, checking the rearview mirror every few seconds.

Before long I noticed a black Jeep on my tail. I tried to see the driver's face, but the Jeep was just far enough away to keep everything a blur. I was certain it was the killer, out to finish me off for good.

In a panic, I reached for my cell phone to call 911. But just then, the Jeep turned off onto a side street.

Thank heavens. A false alarm.

My blood pressure returned from its trip to the stratosphere, and I continued on my way home.

At last I arrived at my street. But as bad luck would have it, there were no parking spaces near my duplex, so I had to park at the other end of the block.

When I got out of my car, I saw something that sent my blood pressure soaring again. I took a look at the car in front of mine and realized I was parked right behind a big black Jeep! For all I knew the killer had taken a shortcut and was lying in wait for me at this very minute.

My heart pounding, I sprinted as fast as could (which isn't saying much) back to my apartment, fully expecting someone to jump out from every passing bush.

I puffed my way up to my front door and, with shaking hands, managed to let myself in.

Quickly flipping the deadbolt, I leaned against the door to catch my breath and then collapsed onto the sofa.

"Oh, Pro!" I moaned. "I just got attacked by a caravan of supermarket carts!"

She gazed down at me from her perch on the bookshelf.

Perhaps someone up there is punishing you for taking away my diamond collar.

Oh, foo. In all the Sturm und Drang of my cart attack, I'd forgotten about Prozac's Kitty Katz Kollar and had left it in my car. No way was I about to go back outside and get it. What if the killer was lurking in my neighbor's azalea bush, just waiting to pounce?

"I bought you a new collar, Pro. Much nicer than that old Tiffany thing. And I'll give it to you first thing in the morning, I promise. But in the meanwhile, won't you please come down? I'll rub your belly for as long as you like. And I've got pepperoni on my breath," I added pleadingly. "You always like that."

But she just rolled over and showed me her tush.

With a weary sigh, I headed for my bedroom and got undressed. Then I brushed my teeth and climbed into bed, but not before checking to make sure all my windows were locked.

I tried watching TV, but even an ancient rerun of *Ozzie and Harriet,* usually a sure fire sleep aid, failed to quell my racing brain.

I couldn't stop thinking about the Attack of the Shopping Carts and wondering who was in that hoodie. It all happened so fast, I hardly even saw my attacker. As far as I knew, it could have been a man or a woman.

Was it Travis, Joy's database thief? Alyce or Barry, her disgruntled clients? Was it wacky Aunt Faith? Or Greg Stanton? Now that I knew about his true credentials as an "artist," had he made up his mind to scare me into silence so he could marry Lady Penelope Ashford?

And what about Cassie? She'd been wearing sweatpants when I stopped by to see her earlier that day. Had she shoved on a matching hoodie and been following me ever since?

But why? As far as I could see, Cassie simply didn't have a motive to kill Joy.

I turned out my bedside lamp and tried to go to sleep, but my cavalcade of suspects kept buzzing in my brain.

Just when I was convinced I was going to be tossing and turning all night, I looked down and saw a lithe little shadow creeping into the room.

Prozac!

My heart flooded with relief as she jumped up on the bed and nuzzled me under my chin.

"Oh, Prozac, honey, I knew you'd come through for

me! Underneath your prickly exterior you've got a heart of gold, after all!"

Yeah, right. Whatever. Where's that belly rub you promised?

She rolled over on her back to get her belly rub, but she couldn't fool me.

The little monster really did care about me.

Her belly rubbed to her satisfaction, she licked my cheek with her sandpaper tongue (no doubt hoping for a wayward scrap of pepperoni), then curled up in a ball under my chin. Her soft fur was like Valium to my frenzied psyche.

At last I was able to relax.

As I lay there on the brink of sleep, I thought back to how it all began—my first day working at Dates of Joy. Random images flashed before my eyes: Joy on her Missing Godiva rant. All those models and actors waiting to interview for a nonexistent part. And Travis in his duct-tape glasses, showing me Joy's Web site—

Omigosh. The Web site!

I sat up with a jolt.

Now I remembered where I'd seen that photo of Cassie's mother—on Joy's client database, when Travis was showing me the Web site.

I'd stopped to admire the photo of an ethereal blonde, a Grace Kelly look-alike, the same blonde I'd seen today in Cassie's bungalow.

Travis told me she'd been a client of Joy's. Had Joy treated her badly, like she'd done with Alyce and Barry? Had Cassie taken the job at Dates of Joy—not to escape the world of hairdressing—but to avenge whatever wrong Joy had done to her mom?

I remembered the tattoo I'd seen earlier on Cassie's shoulder. *Ultio Dulcis Est.*

At the time I'd thought it was a family motto.

Now I got out of bed and fired up my computer.

Seconds later I was typing *Ultio Dulcis Est* into a Google search.

The translation came up instantly:

Revenge Is Sweet.

YOU'VE GOT MAIL!

To: Jausten
From: Shoptillyoudrop
Subject: In My Pocket All Along!

Guess what, darling! I was just cleaning out the pockets of my new Georgie O. Armani jacket before I put it in the wash (That's right, sweetheart! A designer original—and machine washable, too!) when I reached in my pocket and found my Valentine's ring! I must have put it there when I was washing my hands in the ladies' room at Le Chateaubriand.

Which means the Pinkuses didn't steal it after all! Which means your daddy is marching over to Lydia's townhouse with Lester's ring, an apology, and a check for a new plate glass window.

XOXO,
Mom

To: Jausten
From: DaddyO
Subject: A Wee Bit Wrong

Well, Lambchop, it turns out I may have been a wee bit wrong about the Battleaxe stealing your mom's ring. It seems she and her gasbag brother are in the clear this time. But who knows what those two are capable of?

And if Mom thinks I'm going to pay a stranger good money to replace Lester's windowpane when I can do it myself with my Belgian Army Knife and a bit of putty, she's crazy.

I'll head over there tomorrow to take care of the job.

Love 'n' snuggles,
Daddy

Chapter 26

The next morning, after reading about Mom's miraculous recovery of her Valentine's ring from her (machine washable!) Georgie O. Armani jacket, I made my way up the block to my Corolla.

In the bright light of day, my street seemed like a set out of Wisteria Lane. Lots of green grass and lilac bushes and birds chirping gaily in the trees. A far cry from the nightmare alley it had been less than twelve hours ago.

And you can imagine how foolish I felt when I saw a freckle-faced teenager getting into the black Jeep that had sent me running to my apartment in such a panic.

So much for the killer following me home.

I really had to stop overreacting if I expected to continue my career as a part-time semi-professional PI.

At my Corolla, I inspected the dent on my left rear fender. It was rather unsightly, but on the plus side, it matched the dent on my right rear fender.

Eagerly, I grabbed Prozac's Kitty Katz Kollar from the back seat and hurried back to my apartment to show it to her.

"Look what Mommy bought you," I said, waving it under her nose.

A disdainful sniff from Her Majesty.

I don't do rhinestones. And you're not my mommy.

I tried to fasten it around her neck, but all I got for my troubles was a nasty scratch on my wrist.

When last I saw it, she was batting it around like a dead mouse.

Benjamin's was an upscale hair salon in the heart of Brentwood, the kind of place that catered to privileged housewives killing time between Botox shots.

The good news is that I found a parking spot right outside their front door.

The bad news is that Benjamin's receptionist saw me getting out of my freshly dented Corolla.

She blinked in surprise as I walked into the tony salon.

"Hi there," she said, a dewy-eyed twentysomething waiting for her big movie break. "You sure you're not looking for a Supercuts?"

Okay, what she really said was, "How may I help you?" but I could read between the lines.

"I'm here to see Cassie."

"Do you have an appointment?"

"No, but—"

"Sorry," she said, gliding a perfectly manicured fingernail down her schedule sheet. "She's booked all day."

"I just need to talk to her for a few minutes. It's very important."

"How about next Tuesday at ten? Shall I put you down you for a Complete Day of Beauty? If anyone could use one, it's you."

Okay, so she didn't say that last part. But trust me, she was thinking it.

"I can't wait till Tuesday. I need to talk to Cassie now."

And without waiting for permission, I barged into the salon, where I spotted Cassie with a customer.

How odd to see the purple-haired pixie here in the land of Botoxed blondes. But there she was, snipping away at the locks of a brittle forty-something who looked like she was on her way to a DAR meeting.

"Jaine," Cassie cried, catching sight of me. "What are you doing here?"

The starlet/receptionist, who'd been hot on my heels, now piped up: "I told her you were busy, but she wouldn't listen."

"Cassie, we need to talk."

"I can't now, Jaine. I'm with a customer."

"It's about your mom," I whispered. "And Joy Amoroso."

A flush crept up her chalk-white cheeks.

"What's going on?"

I turned to see a tall, skinny guy in a ponytail and designer cowboy gear. From the big brass "B" on his belt buckle, I assumed he was Benjamin.

"Hey," he said, looking me over. "Are you one of the *Don't* models the agency is sending over for my *Beauty Do's & Don'ts* ad?"

"No," I snapped with more than a hint of frost in my voice, "I am not one of your Beauty Don'ts."

Cassie quickly jumped in.

"Jaine's a friend of mine. She just stopped by to pick up something she left in my car."

"Too bad," Benjamin said, walking away. "She'd be a great Don't."

The minute he was gone, Cassie turned to me and hissed, "Wait till I'm through with my client. I'll talk to you then."

So I spent the next twenty minutes in the reception area, getting dirty looks from the starlet/receptionist and leafing through beauty magazines. I particularly enjoyed a hard-hitting piece of journalism entitled "Ten Ways to Get Your Man Excited in Bed."

(The correct answer: Hide the remote.)

Finally Cassie was finished with the DAR lady and hustled me through the salon and out a back door into a narrow alley.

"Make it quick, Jaine. I've only got a few minutes before my next client shows up."

I wasted no time getting to the point.

"I know your mother was one of Joy's former clients. I saw her picture on Joy's database."

"What of it?" she asked, with a defiant tilt of her chin.

"I'm guessing Joy treated her pretty shabbily, just like she treated most of her other clients."

"Shabbily?" She broke out in a bitter laugh. "Joy killed my mother, just as sure as if she'd stuck a knife in her heart."

Slumping down on the salon's back door step, she let out a deep sigh.

"You saw how beautiful my mom was. She wasn't in the movies, but she wanted to be. She tried her hardest, but nothing panned out. Then she got pregnant with me, by some guy she met in one of her acting classes. He broke up with her before I was born and moved to New York. I've never even seen him. Not in person, that is. Although I once caught him in the middle of the night on a Hair Club for Men infomercial.

"Anyhow, Mom worked her fanny off trying to earn enough money for the two of us. One day she saw Joy's ad in the paper. She took every dime she'd saved up and handed it over to Joy, hoping to wind up with some guy who'd take care of both of us. Needless to say, as soon as Joy cashed Mom's check, she wanted nothing more to do with her. She set her up with one or two dates and then hung her out to dry. And when Mom stopped by the office to complain, Joy reamed into her. She told her she was a loser, that her looks were going fast, and that she'd be lucky if she didn't wind up a bag lady.

"Mom was a fragile woman, at her breaking point. And Joy pushed her over the edge. After Joy's tongue-lashing, Mom sank into a deep depression. Three weeks later she killed herself."

Cassie wiped a tear from her cheek with a bony knuckle.

"And so you killed Joy to avenge your mom's death," I said as gently as I could.

She looked up at me, blinking in disbelief.

"Are you crazy? I didn't kill Joy."

"Then why did you go to work for her? You can't expect me to believe you went there simply to take a break from hairdressing."

"I was collecting evidence against her. I kept records of every shady business transaction, every lie she told, every scam she pulled. I wanted to destroy her business. And, if I played my cards right, send her to jail.

"But I didn't kill her. Not that I wouldn't have liked to," she added wistfully. "I just didn't have the nerve."

I didn't know about that. With her tats and nose ring and black leather biker togs, she looked like a pretty tough cookie to me.

"You can't seriously think I poisoned that chocolate?" she asked, sensing my skepticism.

"Maybe just a little," I confessed.

"Oh, for heaven's sakes. It wasn't me. It was Tonio."

So that's who she'd been protecting yesterday.

"Joy was threatening to turn him over to the authorities."

"For driving without a license?"

"No way. It was much more serious than that. I heard her tell him she was going to press criminal charges."

"For what?"

"I don't know. All I know is that she said he'd be spending the next five to ten years behind bars. If that isn't motive for murder, I don't know what is."

So Tonio was lying when he told me Joy had been threatening to report him to the DMV. Last I checked, you don't do five to ten for driving without a license.

"I'm sure Tonio killed Joy to shut her up," Cassie said as she got up to go back into the salon.

And I must confess, I was inclined to agree with her.

Chapter 27

After a pit stop at McDonald's for ~~a Quarter Pounder and fries~~ one of their yummy low-calorie Southwest Salads, I headed over to see Tonio.

According to Cassie, he was still living in Joy's apartment in Westwood. I drove over, taking a chance he'd be home.

There are two kinds of high-rises that line the Wilshire Corridor: Expensive and Ridiculously Expensive. Joy and Tonio's place was one of the more modest affairs.

No circular driveway. No doorman out front. No marble lobby straight from Versailles. Just a simple buzzer at the front entrance.

I buzzed the apartment marked AMOROSO, and seconds later Tonio's gravelly voice came over the line.

"Who is it?"

"Jaine Austen," I called out.

I had a lie all prepped and ready to go: I was there to pay a belated condolence call.

But before I had a chance to roll out my whopper he said, "What a coincidence. I was just about to call you. Come on up. I've got your paycheck."

My paycheck? What a darling man. Surely someone so thoughtful couldn't possibly be a killer, could he?

(I tend to grant automatic sainthood to anyone who hands me a paycheck.)

Tonio greeted me at the door to his fifteenth-floor apartment in jeans and a black T-shirt, the sleeves of which were rolled up to reveal bulging biceps. His normally slicked black hair was tousled and his face was in definite need of a shave.

Very Stanley Kowalski in Mourning.

He led me into a spacious living room with sliding glass doors opening onto a terrace over Wilshire Boulevard. Even fifteen floors up I could hear the traffic whooshing by below.

The place was furnished froufrou ornate, just like Joy's office, chock-a-block with dainty antiques in peaches and pale green. Tonio stood looming against the petite furniture, a hit man in a china shop.

I followed him to the far end of the room, which had been set up as an office area.

Taking a seat behind an ornate desk, he tore a check from a checkbook and handed it to me.

"Joy's business account is tied up in probate, so I'm paying you myself."

Indeed, I looked down and was thrilled to see a check made out to me in the amount of three thousand dollars. From a joint checking account belonging to Joy and Tonio.

"This is really very kind of you," I said.

By now I was feeling like the heel of the century for suspecting him of murder.

"By the way," he asked, as I stood there basking in the glow of my money, "how did you get my address?"

"Cassie gave it to me. I felt bad about not spending more time with you at the memorial service, and I wanted to pay a belated condolence call."

"Oh, right. The memorial service." His eyes clouded over. "That was a pretty rough day."

"How are you holding up?"

"I'm managing," he shrugged.

He picked up a picture of Joy from the desk, the one from her ads, shot through layers of Vaseline, and let out a deep sigh.

"She was the love of my life, and I'm really going to miss her."

Once more I took in his unshaved beard and tousled hair. Clearly he hadn't been taking care of himself. It seemed hard to believe that anyone could actually love Joy, but it looked like Tonio was taking her death pretty hard.

"Thanks for stopping by, Jaine," he said. "I really appreciate it. I'd like to talk some more, but the cleaning lady should be here any minute, and all hell breaks loose once she starts that vacuum."

He got up to walk me to the door.

I hated to do it, after how nice he'd just been, but I couldn't leave without questioning him.

"By the way," I said as we started for the living room, "Cassie told me she heard Joy threatening to turn you over to the police."

He stopped in his tracks and stared at me in disbelief.

"Are you harping on that again? I already told you, she was going to report me to the DMV for driving without a license."

"Cassie said she was going to press criminal charges. And that you'd be serving time in jail."

"I don't know what the hell that girl is talking about. All that purple hair dye must be affecting her brain," he said, shaking his head. "I loved Joy, and she loved me. And she wasn't about to send me off to jail."

His eyes now filled with tears. Which looked pretty genuine.

I was just about to write Cassie off as a goth goofball who'd gotten her facts wrong when a nubile young bimbette came wandering into the living room in mini-shorts and a halter top.

Something told me she was not the cleaning lady.

"Jasmine!" Tonio cried. "I thought I told you to stay in the bedroom."

"I got hungry," she pouted.

I watched as Jasmine sauntered over to the open kitchen area, her fanny jiggling big time in her mini-shorts.

But it wasn't her fanny that caught my eye. It was the honker sapphire earrings dangling from her ears. I'd seen those earrings before. On Joy Amoroso. She'd been wearing them the night she bumped into me and Skip on our very first date from hell.

Several days later, she'd had one of her snit fits when they'd gone missing, convinced someone from her maid service had stolen them. At the time I thought she was overreacting, that she'd probably misplaced them.

But she'd been right. Her earrings *had* been stolen. Not by her maid service, but by Tonio.

"You ripped off Joy's earrings!" I blurted out. "That's why she was going to turn you over to the cops. And that's why you killed her."

"I told you not to wear that bling in public!" Tonio shouted to his bimbette, who was now busy opening a carton of yogurt.

"I'm not in public," she whined. "I'm home with you, sweetpants."

So much for Joy being the love of his life.

And that tousled hair of his had nothing to do with grief. It was bed head!

"Leave us alone, Jasmine," he said through gritted teeth. "I need a moment with Jaine."

"Okay," she shrugged, sashaying back across the living room to a hallway that undoubtedly led to their bedroom love nest.

"Just FYI," she added. "We're almost outta yogurt."

As she disappeared down the hallway, Tonio turned to me.

Gone was the sensitive mourner who'd greeted me at the door. In his place was a fairly intimidating street thug.

"You say I stole those earrings. I say Joy misplaced them and then I found them after she was dead."

He smiled an oily smile that made the hairs on my neck stand on end.

"And what I say goes. Even if it's not exactly the truth."

He then began advancing on me, forcing me to retreat backward with every step he took.

"Yes, Joy was threatening to turn me over to the cops, but I didn't kill her. When I went with Joy to her office to beg her not to turn me in, she ate one of her goddamn Godivas, and the candies were fine then. So the chocolate had to have been poisoned after we got back to the party. And after we got back to the party, your boyfriend Skip had me cornered for the rest of the night, yakking about his dead cat. Which meant I couldn't have poisoned Joy's chocolate."

His face was so close to mine, I could smell the Juicy Fruit on his breath.

"Got that, Sherlock? I couldn't have poisoned the damn chocolate!"

I looked around and suddenly realized I'd backed myself out onto his terrace, fifteen stories above Wilshire Boulevard, the din of traffic loud in my ears.

"If you say a word about the earrings to anybody, you're history. You understand?"

"I understand," I squeaked in a terrified whisper.

By now I could feel the cold metal rail of the balcony pushing into my spine.

I saw Tonio look down at the traffic below and flex his rather formidable biceps. For a frightening instant I wondered if he'd changed his mind and decided to get rid of me for good. One push, and I'd be roadkill.

But I wasn't about to go without a fight. Not now. I had mountains to climb. Flowers to smell. Pizzas to eat.

Before he could make a move, I shoved my way past him, racing back into the living room and out the front door, vowing never again to make accusations against a man with upper arms the size of sandbags.

Chapter 28

The minute I left Tonio, I drove like a maniac to the bank to cash my paycheck. But I was too late. He'd already stopped payment.

Me and my big mouth.

Why couldn't I have been smart enough to accuse him of murder *after* I'd cashed the darn thing?

I drove home, pretty much convinced Tonio killed Joy to stop her from going to the cops. And what about that joint checking account? For all I knew, it was worth a ton of money. Money that Tonio had access to the minute Joy died. Yet another motive for murder.

But what if I was wrong and Tonio was telling the truth? What if he didn't kill her? I remembered Joy eating that chocolate with no ill effects while I was hiding under her desk during her tête-à-tête with Tonio. So whoever slipped the poisoned chocolate in the Godiva box had to have done it after Joy and Tonio had gone back to the party. And I had seen Skip yakking at Tonio most of the night. Was it possible they were together the whole time, as Tonio claimed?

As much as I hated the idea, I knew I'd have to give Skip a call.

Back in my apartment, after fortifying myself with an Oreo or three, I took a deep breath and dialed his number.

He picked up on the first ring. I could just picture him hovering over the phone.

"Jaine, how lovely to hear from you! But why haven't you returned my calls, you naughty girl?"

I haven't mentioned this until now because I wanted to spare you the gooey awfulness of it all, but Skip had been bombarding me with messages, most of them in baby talk, asking Prozac to come over for a play date.

"Sorry, Skip, but I've had a lot on my plate."

"All of it organic, I hope. Ha ha."

"Ha ha," I echoed, forcing a chuckle, and then got down to business.

"I've got something very important I need to ask you about Joy's murder."

"Of course, my dear. I'll be happy to answer your question."

"Great. I need to know—"

"But only in person."

"What?"

"I have to see you and your darling Prozac one more time. I've been missing you both so very much."

"I already told you, Skip. Prozac's not for sale."

Prozac looked up from where she was lounging on my computer keyboard.

I could be for rent, if the price is right.

"Just let me see her this one last time," Skip pleaded, "and I'll answer anything you want to ask."

"Okay," I grudgingly replied. "But promise me. No caviar for Prozac."

"You have my word of honor. No caviar."

Then he urged me to hurry on over.

"I can't wait to see my favorite gal," he gushed. "And you, too, Jaine."

*   *   *

I hung up, dreading the thought of taking Prozac with me to Skip's Malibu manse. It seemed as if she'd finally forgiven me for the whole Diamond Collar Affair, and I didn't want him to do anything to spark her sulk cycle all over again.

But on the plus side, at least the visit would give me a chance to return the collar.

I'd thought about mailing it to him, but was leery about trusting such a valuable bauble with the United States Postal Service, the same folks who've been known to deliver my Christmas cards some time around Flag Day.

I headed to my bedroom closet and reached up to the shelf where I'd hidden the Tiffany box behind a blanket.

Alarm bells started ringing when I saw the blanket had been moved.

Pawing behind the blanket, I found the top of the box. Then the bottom. But no collar.

Frantically I raced to the kitchen for my stepladder to do a thorough search of the shelf. Standing on the ladder, I tossed down every blanket, every sweater, and every shoe box in sight. But the diamond collar was nowhere to be found.

Dammit. Prozac had struck again.

She hadn't forgiven me for taking away her collar. Hell, no. She'd been gloating because she filched the damn thing!

No doubt she'd stashed it away in a hiding spot of her own.

"Prozac!" I cried, storming out into the living room, waving the empty Tiffany box. "Where the heck is the collar??"

She gazed up lazily from where she was lounging on my keyboard.

That's for me to know and you to find out.

I spent the next forty-five minutes ransacking my apartment, checking under pillows and seat cushions, inside old boots, behind P. G. Wodehouse, even raking through Prozac's litter box.

All the while Prozac was following me around, delighted at my antics.

This is way better than The Real Housewives of Beverly Hills.

Finally, in a fit of frustration, I whirled on her.

"If you don't show me where you hid that collar, I swear you'll never get another pizza anchovy as long as you live!"

She could tell I meant business.

After shooting me a filthy look, she led me into the kitchen and plunked herself down next to the trash can.

Of course! The trash can! Prozac's holy grail of leftovers—thanks to my landlord's refusal to fix my garbage disposal. Home of old pizza crusts, moo shu pork slivers, and tuna shards. I can't count the times I'd come home to find the trash can on end, Prozac sniffing around, trolling for snacks.

She'd probably hidden the collar there among her prized pizza crusts.

In a flash I was scrounging around in the garbage, plowing through each and every piece of trash. But, alas, I came up empty-handed. (If you don't count a free cereal sample I'd thrown out by mistake.)

I was sitting there, feeling quite dejected, trying to get up the energy to wash my hands so I could eat my free cereal, when suddenly I heard the sound of a truck coming down the street.

Not just any truck. The garbage truck.

Omigosh! It was garbage day. And suddenly I wondered: What if Prozac hid the collar in a bag of garbage I'd *already* brought out to the curb?

I had to stop the truck before they carted it away!

Racing outside, I groaned to see the giant truck pulling up right outside my duplex.

I got there just as the automated arm of the truck was hoisting up my black garbage can.

"Stop!" I shrieked to the driver. "Let my garbage go!"

The garbage man, a wiry guy with a toothpick dangling from his mouth, looked down at me from the height of his cab.

"Say what?"

"Please put down my trash can. There may be a diamond collar in there."

"A diamond collar?" he asked, shifting the toothpick to the other side of his mouth.

"Yes. From Tiffany's. My cat threw it away by mistake."

"Your *cat* threw away your diamond collar?"

"Actually, it's hers, not mine."

"You bought your cat a diamond collar? From Tiffany's?" He shook his head in disgust. "Only in Beverly Hills."

"No, no, it was a gift from an infuriating old codger who made me have a picnic lunch with his dead mother and got into a fight with a blind jazz pianist and offered me twenty-five thousand dollars for Prozac. My cat was mad at me for not letting her keep the collar, and at first I thought she'd forgiven me, but no way, she's not the forgiving kind. Why, she once sulked for three straight weeks after I tried to give her a bath, something I'll never try again, that's for sure. Anyhow, she found the collar where I hid it in the closet and then she hid it somewhere else, and I've searched everywhere in the apartment even behind P. G. Wodehouse but it wasn't there, so I'm guessing she stashed it in the trash because that's where she always goes digging for snacks."

As I may have mentioned, I tend to babble under stress.

The garbage man just sat there chewing on his toothpick.

Finally, he said: "The guy offered you twenty-five grand for some Prozac? Hasn't he ever heard of generics?"

"Look, it's all very confusing. Can't I please just have my garbage back?"

"All right, lady."

And much to my eternal relief, he released the can to the ground. "Just one more thing," he called out as he drove off down the street. "You might want to try some of your friend's Prozac. Sure looks like you could use some."

Alone with my garbage, I wasted no time diving in.

Soon I was elbow deep in old pizza crusts and banana peels—not to mention Skip's appalling soy-carob pie. I continued burrowing my way through all sorts of glop until at last, plunging my arm into a mass of sodden moo shu pork, I felt something hard.

With a small prayer to the jewelry gods, I pulled it up.

Hallelujah! It was the diamond collar, shards of moo shu pork clinging to its clasp.

Clutching it to my heart, I started up the path to my apartment.

Just as I was passing Lance's place, he came bounding out his front door, looking springtime fresh in chinos and a gingham checked shirt, a pullover tied around his shoulders, very Ralph Lauren in the Hamptons.

"Jaine, sweetie," he tsked, plucking a pizza crust from my shoulder. "You've really got to stop these between meal snacks. And a little deodorant wouldn't hurt either," he added, taking a whiff of my eau de garbage.

"I was just rooting around in the garbage for a diamond collar," I explained.

"That's nice, hon," he said, lost, as he often is, in Lance World. "So how do I look? Marvelous, I know. You'll never guess where I'm going. Donny's taking me for a drive up to Santa Barbara in his new Porsche! Isn't that exciting? Oh! There he is now!"

And indeed, parked at the curb right beyond my garbage can was a shiny silver Porsche convertible, with a James Dean–ish hottie behind the wheel.

"Ciao, sweetie!" Lance cried with a jaunty wave.

As he scurried down the path, his blond curls bobbing in the breeze, I returned to my apartment, where the mood was distinctly less sunny.

"Prozac!" I growled, waking her from one of her gazillion daily naps. "Do you realize what hell you just put me through?"

She yawned mightily as I waved the moo shu–crusted collar in her face.

"What have you got to say for yourself, young lady?"

She looked up at me with wide green eyes.

Can I have some of that pork?

Chapter 29

"Jaine, my dear. What took you so long?"

Skip stood at the front door of his Casa de One Percenters, a palatial hacienda in the hills of Malibu.

"I got held up with a few things," I said, sparing him the details of my garbage dive.

It had taken me a good half hour to scrub myself—and the collar—clean in the shower. Another half hour to get dressed and lure Prozac into her cat carrier. And yet another forty minutes of non-stop wailing (from me—at the traffic) before finally making it over to Skip's place.

Now he ushered me into a vestibule the size of my living room. The first thing I saw, hanging in a nook above an occasional table, was a framed oil painting of a cat who bore a remarkable resemblance to Prozac.

Miss Marple, I presumed.

Skip was kneeling on the floor, entranced with her doppelgänger.

"How's my darling Prozac?" he cooed, eagerly unlatching the door to her carrier and gathering her in his arms. "Do you remember me, sweetums?"

Prozac took a disdainful sniff.

Oh, hell. It's old Denture Breath.

"Won't you join me in the den, my dear?" Skip said

to me, finally remembering I was alive. "I was just about to watch some home movies of Miss Marple."

I followed him down a hallway along priceless Persian rugs, past rooms furnished with museum-quality pieces and velvet drapes straight out of *Gone With the Wind*.

At last we arrived at his den, a wood-paneled affair with worn leather furniture and hunting prints on the walls. An old-fashioned projector had been set up on an end table facing a screen on the far wall.

"Do sit down," he said, gesturing to a leather sofa, permanently indented with ancestral tush marks. "I had my housekeeper set out some snacks."

There on a coffee table in front of the sofa was a platter of highly unappetizing munchies: celery sticks, radishes, eggplant puree, and some unidentifiable slimy white globs.

"Those are tofu balls," Skip explained, following my gaze, "with carrot puree in the center."

Lordie, where's a barf bag when you need one?

"I made them myself," he grinned proudly. "You'll have to try one."

Not without a court order.

"And look what I've got for my precious Prozac!" He held up a bowl of succulent white morsels. "Chopped lobster tail!"

Prozac's eyes grew large with lust.

Way to go, Denture Breath!

"Skip," I protested. "You promised you wouldn't feed her fancy food."

"I promised I wouldn't feed her caviar. You didn't say anything about lobster."

And before I could stop him, he had Prozac in his lap, hand-feeding her lobster tidbits.

Oh, hell. I'd never get her back on cat food now.

"Have some alfalfa juice," he said, handing me a glass of murky green liquid.

"Yum," I said, taking a nauseating sip.

Then I reached into my purse for the Tiffany collar.

"Skip, I've been meaning to return this to you." I held it out to him, praying it didn't smell of moo shu pork. "I can't keep it."

"Oh, but you must. I insist. You'll make an old man very happy."

He gazed at me with earnest watery eyes.

Oh, what the heck. I'd keep it. Whatever he paid for it was probably chump change for him. And after all my dates from hell with the guy, I deserved it.

"Thank you so much," I said, slipping it back in my purse.

I was sitting there, trying to decide what to do with the money I got when I sold it—New car? New TV? Membership in the Pie of the Month Club?—when a stout, middle-aged gal with a cast-iron perm popped her head in the door.

"I'm leaving now, Mr. Skip."

"All right, Yolanda."

"I've got your dinner warming in the oven. Cheese-free, gluten-free vegetarian lasagna."

No cheese? No meat? Gluten-free pasta? Talk about leeching all the fun from lasagna.

"See you tomorrow, Mr. Skip."

And off she went (lucky gal), her footsteps echoing down the corridor.

As soon as she'd gone, Skip turned to me and winked.

"Alone at last."

Oh, hell. I had to stop this love train, pronto, before it left the station.

"So anyhow, Skip," I said, in my most businesslike voice, "about Joy's murder—"

"Must we talk about that now? Can't we watch *The Adventures of Miss Marple?* I really wanted you to see it."

"Okay, sure," I sighed. The guy'd just given me a diamond collar. The least I could do was sit through some movies of his dead cat.

So for the next fifteen minutes I watched Miss Marple napping, scratching, and playing with a ball of yarn.

Eat your heart out, Steven Spielberg.

"Look," cried Skip excitedly, just as I was about to embark on a little nap of my own. "Here she is, using the toilet to make poo poo."

And indeed, there on the screen was Miss Marple, sitting on a toilet seat, doing her business.

"That's amazing!" I said.

Prozac looked up from her lobster bits and eyed the screen, unimpressed.

Yeah, but could she cough up a hair ball the size of a kumquat?

We continued to watch Miss Marple in action—wearing a Santa hat, dressed in a kitty tutu, and sitting behind the wheel of Skip's Bentley. Somewhere in the middle of one of Miss Marple's antics, Prozac gobbled up the last of the lobster bits and started yowling for more.

"Is my precious princess still hungry?" Skip asked. "Let Daddy get you a refill."

"Please, Skip," I said as he started to get up. "She's had more than enough."

Prozac shot me a dirty look.

Mind your own beeswax!

"A little more won't hurt her," Skip said.

And before I could stop him, he'd turned off the projector and was out the door.

I glanced down at the vegan munchies on the coffee table. How totally unfair that Prozac was getting lobster tails and I was stuck with those ghastly tofu blobs. It had been ages since I'd scarfed down my Quarter Pounder (I mean, Southwest Salad) at McDonald's, and by now I was starving.

No way was I about to dig into the tofu blobs, so I rummaged around my purse and was thrilled to discover half a Hershey's bar stuck in a tissue packet.

Just as I was unwrapping it and plucking a piece of lint off the *H*, Skip came back with Prozac's lobster.

He took one look at the Hershey's bar and froze dead in his tracks.

"My God!" he cried. "Are you crazy?"

Then he sprang to life, wrenching it from my hand.

"Don't you realize this is poison?" he said, waving the chocolate bar in my face.

Okay, that did it. I'd had it up to here with this health nut.

"For your information," I said, grabbing the Hershey's bar right back, "I happen to eat chocolate all the time, and I'm perfectly healthy."

"Who cares about you?" he screeched. "I was talking about Prozac. Chocolate is poisonous to cats. That's how poor Miss Marple died. Some idiot fed her chocolate!"

He stood there, eyes popping, the veins on his temple pulsing, his face flushed with fury.

And suddenly I flashed back to my first date with Skip at the steak restaurant, when Joy came over to our table and rambled on about how much she'd adored Miss Marple, how she'd fed her tuna and caviar and truffles. Omigosh! When Joy said she'd fed Miss Marple truffles, had she meant the chocolate kind? From her Godiva box?

Was it possible that, however unwittingly, Joy had killed Miss Marple?

Clearly Skip had been cuckoo over his dearly departed cat. Cuckoo enough to have killed Joy to avenge Miss Marple's death?

One look at his wild eyes and throbbing temples convinced me that he was.

When Joy bragged about feeding Miss Marple those truffles, she'd undoubtedly signed her own death warrant.

Skip was watching me closely now, as if he realized he'd said too much.

I had to get the hell out of there, but I couldn't leave without Prozac.

Skip had her firmly in his grasp, back on the sofa, feeding her lobster bits, cooing to her in a high-pitched keen that made me feel sick inside. I couldn't risk grabbing her; Lord only knew how he might harm her in a struggle.

Somehow I had to convince him I suspected nothing, and then break away to call 911.

"I'm so sorry about Miss Marple," I said, trying my best to sound soothing. "I don't blame you for being upset. And you're so right. I'll never eat chocolate in front of Prozac again."

The tension seemed to drain from his face.

"So sorry I raised my voice, my dear," he said with an apologetic smile.

Thank goodness he seemed to be mollified.

"Ready for more Adventures of Miss Marple?" he asked.

"Absolutely. But first, I need to use the powder room. That alfalfa juice just zipped right through me."

"Of course. It's the third door to your left."

I grabbed my purse and headed out the door as calmly as I could. Then as soon I was in the hallway, I dashed into the first room I saw.

At first I thought it was a child's room, with a pink

canopy bed and bins of toys everywhere. But then I saw
a plushly carpeted scratching post and realized the walls
were lined with framed photos of the cat I'd seen in the
vestibule. An open closet door revealed tiny cat outfits
hanging from the rod.

Good heavens, the room was a shrine to Miss
Marple!

But I couldn't stand around pondering Skip's obses-
sion with a dead cat.

I had to get help.

I whipped out my cell phone. But just as I was about
to call 911, the phone rang.

Damn. Of all times for someone to call.

I checked the caller ID but didn't recognize the number.

"Who is it?" I snapped, pressing the TALK button.

"It's me. Lance! Oh, Jaine. The most horrible thing
has happened."

"I can't talk now, Lance."

I didn't have time to stand around listening to a tragic
tale of how he got a stain on his Ralph Lauren sweater.

"But, Jaine. I'm in jail!"

"Jail??"

"Yes, it turns out Donny's a kleptomaniac. All those
gifts he gave me were stolen. And so was his new
Porsche. I got arrested as an accessory to Grand Theft
Auto, and I need you to come and bail me out."

"I will as soon as I can, but right now I'm trapped
with a killer and I've got to call the cops."

"Trapped with a killer? That's awful! If you make it
out alive, you won't forget to bail me out, will you?"

"No, I won't forget."

"And would you mind bringing me a turkey wrap
from the Urth Café, hold the mayo, no chips?"

Arggh! It would serve him right if I let him rot in cus-
tody.

"Gotta go," I snapped, clicking him to oblivion. Then, with trembling fingers, I called 911. My heart was in my stomach as I waited for them to pick up. It was taking forever. Why, oh, why did I have to live in a city with so many emergencies? I just prayed they wouldn't put me on hold. I was standing there waiting for an operator to come on the line, imagining Lance giving fashion tips to his cellmates, when suddenly I felt the phone being ripped from my hand.

I whirled around to see Skip standing there, madness gleaming in his watery blue eyes.

With surprising strength, he hurled the phone across the room. It landed with a crash behind the scratching post. I was certain he'd broken it.

Then I glanced down and saw what looked like a giant hypodermic needle in his hand. Cripes, that thing looked dangerous. And something told me he wasn't there to give me a flu shot.

"This was *her* room," he was saying. "Isn't it beautiful? Nothing was too good for Miss Marple. She was the love of my life. And that bitch Joy took her away from me."

His face flushed with rage under his ghastly toupee.

"I brought Miss Marple with me to Joy's office one day when I was having new photos taken," he said, his eyes glazing over at the memory. "Joy said she'd play with her while I was in the photo studio. That night Miss Marple got sick. She died before I could even get her to the vet. I had no idea Joy fed her anything.

"For months, I just assumed Miss Marple's death was an unexplained tragedy. But then that night in the restaurant when Joy bragged about feeding Miss Marple truffles, my heart stopped. I remembered those Godiva truffles in Joy's office, and I realized that dreadful woman had poisoned my precious angel with her chocolates!"

He smiled now, a soft faraway smile.

"So you see, I had to kill her."

"Of course, you did," I clucked in false sympathy, wondering how the hell I could make it past him without getting stabbed by that godawful needle.

"I was afraid you figured it out," he said. "Tonio called and told me you were snooping around. He was lying to you, of course. We weren't together all night at the Valentine's party. Tonio left me for about ten minutes to go to the men's room. But he was so frightened the police would try to pin the murder on him, he begged me to give him an alibi. I was only too happy to oblige, since I was the one who put that poisoned chocolate in Joy's Godiva box. While Tonio went to the men's room, I hurried across to her office, tossed out the other chocolates, and slipped in my little poisoned gift. I wanted Joy to die just like my poor Miss Marple did.

"I thought I got away with it. But now you know the truth. So it's time for you to go. The same way Joy did. And Nancy Ruth."

"Nancy Ruth?"

"My wife. We were married fifty-two years. Enough was enough."

No doubt about it. The guy was a certified fruitcake.

"It won't hurt much if you don't struggle," he said, waving the giant needle.

"What the hell is that thing?" I asked.

"It's my flavor injector. You can buy it at any cooking supply store. It's how I injected the poison in Joy's chocolate. I used it today to stuff the tofu balls with carrot puree. Now, of course, it's filled with cyanide."

He started slowly toward me, his flavor injector aimed straight at my gut.

Oh, how I wanted to shove him aside and make a run for it! But I couldn't risk getting stabbed.

Then I realized I was still carrying my purse. Reaching inside, I felt around for my Aqua Net, prepared to zap Skip in the eyes and render him helpless. But when I pulled out the can, I realized it wasn't hair spray—but Squirrel-B-Gone, the stuff I'd used to ward off Rocky and Bullwinkle. I just prayed it would work on humans, too. Aiming straight for his eyes, I gave it a spritz.

And out came . . . nothing.

Dammit. The plastic safety guard was still on!

Why do they make these things so hard to open, anyway? Don't the people at Squirrel-B-Gone realize their customers might someday find themselves face to face with a geriatric maniac?

With no time to fiddle with the safety guard, I simply lobbed the can of Squirrel-B-Gone at Skip's head.

The bad news is I missed. But the good news is he was so startled, he dropped his flavor injector.

My cue to get the hell out of there.

Wasting no time, I went charging out into the hall.

And that's when fate stepped in and slipped me a knuckleball.

I hadn't taken two steps when I tripped over one of Skip's precious Persian rugs.

Dammit.

The next thing I knew I was sprawled on the floor, Skip straddling my chest, pinning my arms to my sides with his legs. For a skinny guy, he felt awfully heavy.

Then, with a sinking feeling in the pit of my stomach, I saw his flavor injector peeking out from his shirt pocket.

"Look, Skip. There's no need to kill me. Honest. I swear I won't tell a soul that you killed Joy. I hated her, too. It'll be our little secret."

"Sorry, Jaine. I can't take that chance. And besides, I really do want Prozac, and I don't think I'll get her unless you're out of the picture."

"So," he said, baring his dentures in a feral grin, "I'll just kill two birds with one flavor injector."

He took it out of his pocket with a flourish.

Squirming mightily, I tried to free my arm to punch him in the groin, but he was a lot tougher than he looked.

As much as I struggled, I couldn't break free.

Now I cringed to see the syringe coming closer and closer. Skip was aiming it straight for my neck.

He was *thisclose* to plunging it in when suddenly a giant furball with lobster breath came hurtling through the air and sank her teeth into Skip's hand.

Thank heavens! My darling Prozac had come to my rescue!

That's what I'd like to think, anyway. Frankly, I suspect she was just trying to snag lobster bits from Skip's fingers.

Whatever the reason, Skip dropped the flavor injector, yowling in pain. At last I managed to free my arms and gave him that punch in the groin he so richly deserved.

Shoving him off me, I left him doubled over, clutching his privates. Then I grabbed the flavor injector and raced back to Miss Marple's room.

I scrambled to pick up my cell phone from where Skip had hurled it behind the scratching post. Not only was it still working, but an operator had actually come on the line and heard Skip confessing to Joy's murder.

I quickly gave her Skip's address and minutes later heard the wail of police sirens. Soon the cops were storming in the front door. After kindly fixing Skip an ice pack for his groin, they carted him off to the Crazy Old Coot wing of the county jail.

The minute he was gone, I turned to Prozac and gathered her in my arms.

"Thank you, my precious angel, for saving my life!"

She gazed up at me with wide, adoring eyes.

It's the least I could do for someone as wonderful as you.

Okay, so technically, she jumped down and trotted back to the den to lick the last of the lobster from the bowl.

But a cat owner can dream, can't she?

YOU'VE GOT MAIL!

To: Jausten
From: Shoptillyoudrop
Subject: Just Got Back from the Hospital

Hi, sweetheart—Just got back from the hospital. Don't get alarmed. It's nothing serious. Daddy cut himself with his Belgian Army Knife trying to replace Lydia's windowpane and had to have a few stitches taken. Frankly I hope it will teach him a lesson. He's resting in bed right now.

I took that dratted knife away from him and will throw it away just as soon as I finish using the corkscrew to open a bottle of chardonnay.

I just hope we're not out of Oreos.

Love and XXX,
Mom

To: Jausten
From: DaddyO
Subject: Minor Mishap

Dearest Lambchop—

After a minor mishap with my Belgian Army Knife, Mom has decided to throw it away. It's all for the best, really. The quality of the cutting blade, I must confess, was really rather shoddy.

Which is why I just sent away for the new, improved Belgian Army Knife, Imperial Officer's Edition, complete with built-in toenail clippers.

It should be here tomorrow.

Love 'n' snuggles from,
Daddy

Epilogue

Skip Holmeier fans will be happy to learn that, thanks to a successful insanity plea, he is now residing at a luxury sanitarium for the criminally cuckoo. Last I heard, he'd fallen madly in love with the sanitarium cat, Irving, whom he insists on calling Miss Marple.

I never did get to cash in on my Tiffany collar. When I brought it in to be appraised, it turned out to be a fake! To think that I almost swan dived into a garbage truck to rescue that thing. Oh, well. Lesson learned, class. Never accept jewelry from a tofu-eating homicidal maniac.

The police dropped all charges against Lance once they realized Donny had been acting alone in his kleptomania. Stinging from yet another romance gone bad, Lance swore off men forever. A vow he kept for a whole three and a half days, before falling head over heels for a guy he met at a "Who Needs Men, Anyway?" workshop.

Business is booming for Travis, the computer nerd-turned-matchmaker. In a stroke of marketing genius and/or generosity, he fixed up all Joy's unhappy clients with free dates, which generated so much goodwill, he wound up with tons of new referrals. Now he has fancy new offices just off Rodeo Drive, where he always keeps an open box of Godiva chocolates for his clients to enjoy.

Greg Stanton fessed up about his Uncle George's paintings and spent three months in prison for art fraud. While serving time, he penned his memoirs, which are now being made into a major motion picture starring George Clooney as Greg and Sean Connery as "Uncle George."

And Barry, the fountain pen nerd? You're not going to believe this (I sure didn't), but he's engaged to Albany, the model, whom he bumped into at a fountain pen collectors convention. It turns out Albany is a fountain pen fanatic, just like Barry. They plan to name their first child Parker Esterbrook.

In other romance news, Alyce Winters is seeing a guy she met on Travis's Web site, an orthodontist from Encino. And rumor has it that Cassie is dating Carl, the ex-con from Frugal Fixin's.

As for Aunt Faith, she opened a jewelry shop in Santa Monica, where her wacky baubles soon became all the rage. She's now selling her stuff on the Home Shopping Channel.

My mom is one of her biggest customers.

And you'll never guess who pushed those shopping carts at me at Pet Palace. Muriel, the clerk! Turns out she had some pretty serious anger management issues. But after months of therapy, she's much better. Last I heard, she's working at the post office.

Prozac's the same as ever, the queen of all she surveys. I finally weaned her off caviar and lobster tails. Now she's into baby lamb chops.

Oh, and one more thing. I got the craziest letter in the mail the other day. I thought I'd die when I read it. Here's what it said:

Hi, there!
I've really enjoyed chatting with you. I think
you're cute and funny. Would you like to go out
with me Saturday night?
Det. *Scott Willis*

That's right. It was from Detective Adam's Apple (aka Scott Willis)! When he showed it to me for my approval, I assumed he was going to send it to a petite blonde he'd met online. But no, the gal he'd fallen for was not some petite blonde, but moi!

Oops. There's the doorbell. That's him now.

Wish me luck!